Copyright ©

All rights reserved

The characters and events portrayed in this book are fictitious. Any similarity to real persons, living or dead, is coincidental and not intended by the author.

No part of this book may be reproduced, or stored in a retrieval system, or transmitted in any form or by any means, electronic, mechanical, photocopying, recording, or otherwise, without express written permission of the publisher.

ISBN: 9798328422086

D. A Marsh

*For the mum that chose me and
always supported me*

CHAPTER 1

Sitting at the dining table facing the window of his rental flat on Edinburgh's Royal Mile trawling through news reports on his phone Alex Mackintosh sips at his coffee hoping to see something about his parents who have been missing since their plane crashed in the Peruvian jungle, the plane was found with the pilot still in his seat, but there isn't much more than that, no other bodies were found. The wreck was found scattered over a large area of dense jungle and having crashed through the trees, breaking up on the way it's been almost impossible to find anything but scraps amongst the trees and dense vegetation. News has been slow getting through with communications difficult between the Peruvian government and the UK. Getting up and having a stretch he walks up to the window looking out at a miserable view of a rain-soaked Edinburgh.

Thinking about what he wants to do, with the days starting to blend into one since he left his role as a nuclear physicist for the European

Space Agency, having taken extended leave after hearing about his parents, feeling at a crossroads and needing some time to clear his head a little before returning to normal life. His relationship with his parents had always been difficult, as soon as he was old enough, he was sent to a boarding school in Edinburgh and spent all of his formative years there, which in hindsight was probably the reason he has been as successful as he has been, always seeking approval, but he always thought he had time. Always thinking of himself as an outcast and spent his time either with his head in books or asleep which eventually led to a successful career having worked for both NASA and the ESA, never quite fulfilling his dream of going to space, but he found that his research and projects got him close enough to be happy. Sitting back at his dining table looking around his open plan kitchen/lounge he starts to realise just how little he has despite having well paid jobs, he's never been a materialistic person and he's always been away somewhere for work making it rare that he spends time in the flat that he rents.

Just as he's about to make another coffee the buzzer for the 3rd floor flat snaps him out of his daydream, walking over and looking at the camera, just the postman, so he buzzes him up. Not many people make it past the buzzer but the postman is one that always does, mainly thanks to online shopping, which he's pretty sure his neighbour's hate him for since he's rarely around during the day to answer the door. Standing at the door looking through the spyhole waiting for the postman to appear he tries to work out what it is since he hasn't ordered anything this time. He opens the door to be greeted by a soaked postman and a recorded delivery brown envelope from London with a nice solicitor's stamp on the front. Signing for the letter and thanking the postman he walks slowly back to the table looking at the solicitor's stamp with a sinking feeling in his gut, either he's done something wrong or it's about his parents.

Sitting down at the dining table he takes a mouthful of coffee before he even considers opening the envelope. Ripping the envelope open, reading the first line he almost spits his coffee all over the table, the reading of the last will and testament of William and Elizabeth Mackintosh. Reading through the rest of the letter, it goes on to explain that since it's been six months since the crash his parents are now deemed to have died in the accident. Going through the rest of the letter which appears to have taken a little longer to arrive than it should have, he has been asked to attend the reading on Monday 11th January at the solicitors London office, which had he been working could have been an issue, but since he's not exactly busy at the moment he decides to start looking at flights, not wanting to sit on a train for 7 hours probably with some spotty adolescent idiot playing his music too loud and of course the customary screaming brat kicking the back of his chair all the way to London and of course the issue that despite being able to drive he's never actually owned a car. He finds a flight for Sunday morning and books business class, not sure how long he'll be in London he only books a one-way flight.

Flight booked, he starts to wonder what if anything they would have had to leave him, most of the time they spent travelling collecting artifacts from ancient ruins that they have discovered on the way, appearing regularly in magazines or in documentaries on Nat Geo or Discovery. Putting thoughts of what could be to the back of his mind for now he starts gathering a few clothes together and anything else he might need to take with him, being sure to put his passport in the bag, it wouldn't be the first time he's forgotten it. Finishing packing his bag and zipping it up leaving it by the front door ready to go Sunday morning, he suddenly remembers a box of postcards and letters they have sent over the years, probably the only real memories he has of his parents, taking the box out of the cupboard he decides to put the letters and postcards in his bag, maybe something sentimental to take with him, since that's about all he's seen of his parents since graduating with honours from Edinburgh University. Still being relatively young for the number of letters after his name at 32. Alex doesn't really feel sad about his parents, often they seemed more like acquaintances rather than family, the sort of people you hear from a couple times of year at birthdays, Christmas and funerals. Funerals less so since his family are pretty scattered and rarely stay in touch.

Having done everything that he needs to do for the day he decides to go for a walk making sure he's got a warm coat on and a scarf because January in Edinburgh can be pretty damn cold. Walking out of his flat he starts a slow walk up the Royal Mile looking for somewhere for a drink and some lunch, not really being one to cook, normally just takeaways and meals out, table for one please. Spotting one of his favourite places to eat because it's normally fairly quiet during the day and not far from home, he walks into the Inn on the Mile, getting a drink he heads straight toward the back, a nice quiet corner, taking a drink of beer while staring at the menu not sure what he wants or if he even wants food yet, he just sits with his drink, which is pretty much how Friday and Saturday go, a few drinks and sat watching Marvel films passing the time until his alarm wakes him up Sunday morning.

Making a coffee and booking a taxi to the airport, he double checks his bag, finishes his coffee and goes to wait outside, the taxi arriving just as he steps out into a nice fresh -1 Celsius

Edinburgh. The taxi ride was uneventful, no one in their right mind is out at 7am on a Sunday morning, unless that is they haven't made it home from Saturday night. Arriving at the airport, which thanks to covid is deadly quiet at the moment, he makes his way through check-in with half an hour till his flight starts boarding. He does what he always does and finds a seat as far away from anyone else as he possibly can, a habit that has nothing to do with covid, he just doesn't really like people and people in airports just seem to want to talk for no reason. Looking through the day's news on his phone when he stumbles across an article about his parents, reading through the article he doesn't see anything new to him until he looks at the picture of them seemingly in their London apartment surrounded by glass display cases with artefacts and trinkets from around the world, a photo he's never seen before. I guess at least now he knows what he might inherit. Not noticing the time go past he jumps as the call comes over the PA for boarding, jumping up and walking toward the gate and quickly making his way onto the plane and into his seat the first thing he starts thinking about is more coffee. Sitting looking out of the window as the plane starts off down the runway for take-off, he keeps looking at the seat belt light, waiting for it to go off so that the hostess will come around with coffee. Finally, the light goes off and the hostesses spring into action and Alex is happy again with his coffee in hand.

The flight itself goes by without much happening landing in London at around 10.30am thankfully the weathers a little warmer than Edinburgh and although 5oc isn't exactly warm compared to Edinburgh it's almost like spring after the winter in Edinburgh. Making his way off the plane and through the airport, he hails a taxi to get to a hotel near the solicitor's office, watching London go by out of the taxi window, he realises it's been a few years since he's been in London, but nothing has really changed, nothing really does in London.

Arriving at his hotel a little before 12pm he thanks the taxi driver and heads inside straight to reception, booking a nice room on the top floor so he can sit and at least have a reasonable view of London while he's here. Sitting down looking out of the window, he starts to think about what he wants to do now he's here, not really having any plans he decides to just go for a walk, find somewhere to have a drink and some decent food and just pass Sunday by like that. Finding a quiet bar, he pulls the letter from his jacket pocket, 10am in the morning he'll be the proud owner of a bunch of artefacts that he has no idea what to do with, apart from maybe donate them to a museum, christ there's enough there to open his own museum. Passing Sunday quietly he decides to head to the hotel for some sleep since times creeping up 10pm, making his way back to his room he leaves the letter and his passport on the table to pick up on his way out in the morning and heads to bed with an alarm for 8am to make sure he has time for at least two coffees. It takes two before he can think about moving.

Waking up Monday morning and making his first coffee, he realises he has an unusual feeling in the pit of his stomach, nerves, he never gets nervous so why now? Pushing it to the back of his mind he sits and drinks his 2nd coffee before he starts the slow walk round to the solicitors which is only two streets away from the hotel, stepping out of the hotel is a bit of a shock to the system, the hotel has been a nice consistent, comfortable temperature, outside on the other hand feels like he woke up in the Arctic. Not wasting much time, he takes a quicker than normal walk to the solicitor's office, not wanting to be outside any longer than necessary.

Walking into the office he looks around at something that would fit perfectly into a Dickens novel. The minute he steps in he hears an older voice coming from behind the reception desk "Mr Mackintosh? Mr. Rosenthal is waiting for you" answering the woman that the voice belongs to quietly thinking that she could be in a museum as well, her age seems to goes against anything possible. He's ushered straight into his parent's solicitor's office with Mr Rosenthal thanking his receptionist Dorothy, which is so full oak it could have wiped out a forest, not to mention the solicitor who almost looks the same shade of brown as the wood, too many hours under a sunbed? Or too many holidays in the sun? Being careful not to let a laugh out he sits down in front of the desk while the mahogany man in front of him shuffles through a pile of papers. Finally finding the one he wants he instantly starts reading his parents will out in a very matter of fact, well-rehearsed tone. Nothing too surprising to start, the normal legal jargon that goes with anything like this, witnessed by the 200-year-old receptionist. Then the shocks come, sitting only paying half attention to the solicitor, having already switched off to the monotone voice. First comes the bit he'd guessed, all of the artefacts and possessions in the apartment, then the first shock, his parents owned the apartment which is valued at £2.5million. The solicitors voice not changing or wavering then goes onto his parent's finances and the £15million they have in the bank which because Alex is the sole beneficiary is now his. Everything else goes straight over his head, signing bits of paper and being told the keys for the apartment will be ready in the morning for him to collect and the rest of the paperwork will be completed then. Walking straight outside thankful for the cold air now, something to stop him collapsing, he walks straight into the first open bar that he sees and orders a beer and whisky, his hands shaking following his meeting and the news that he is now a multi-millionaire.

CHAPTER 2

Having finished his drinks and not feeling particularly hungry he decides to take a slow walk back to the hotel. It's a slow walk with his head spinning, he's always earned enough money to allow him to do what he wants, but now he has millions he has no idea what to think or do. Reaching the hotel via a shop to get some beer and heading straight up to his room, he sits at the table trying to work out what he wants to do, it's only 1pm and he can't really do anything until tomorrow, when he can start making decisions about his parent's apartment and everything in it, he can't do much without the keys.

Getting a can of beer and sitting at the table with his laptop, he starts looking into what his parents had been doing closer to the accident hoping come across something he hasn't already seen, to do with all the artefacts in the glass display cases. Looking through articles finding the normal ones, a few pages in magazines, Nat Geo, Discover Magazine and such, one article in the Smithsonian that makes him laugh as his mind wanders back to the old receptionist at the solicitor's office. One report about a £2million donation to cancer research that he hadn't seen before, but nothing that stands out. Sitting staring at his laptop, drinking his beer he realises that he's not going to find much information he doesn't already know, he always tried to keep up with what his parents were doing with little interest, his mind has always been set on the future not so much looking into the past.

Grabbing his bag and pulling out the box of postcards and letters, which thankfully his ocd mans they are all in order, sorted by date. Looking at the last one, there's not much written on it, which is normal, but the postcard is from Sedona, Arizona which looks like the last place they visited before Peru. Closing his laptop and putting the postcard down, he grabs his jacket and decides he needs some air and heads back outside for a walk, for some reason heading for Russell Square, he's always liked the park there. Leaving the hotel and making his way to Hyde Park station not needing to look at the map after spending time in London in the past, he heads straight for the Piccadilly Line to Russell Square thankful that due to the pandemic even the London underground is quiet these days and personal space is something that people actually understand at last. Now they treat each other like they've got the plague, which leads Alex to considering buying a plague doctors mask, then having to stifle a laugh, not wanting to look like Joaquin Pheonix as the joker. Arriving at Russell Square station he starts the walk toward the escalators breathing a heavy sigh as he realises all the escalators are out of order. Standing staring up the flight of steps he begrudgingly starts the slow climb to freedom, reaching the top and smelling the London air again he remembers a pub nearby and starts the walk round needing to sit and have a drink before he walks anywhere else, Alex isn't exactly the fittest person on the planet, sitting at a desk all the time the most exercise he gets is lifting a coffee cup. Stepping through the doors of the Shakespeare's Head to that familiar aroma of stale beer and musk of old man remembering all the misspent time at university, all those Monday morning lectures after weekends of drinking, having to catch up for the ones he couldn't remember through his hangover's. Ordering a beer and a mixed grill thinking that food at some point would be a good idea he finds a quiet corner, one thing he always does is scan the room on the way in for opportunities.

Sitting quietly sipping his beer he starts thinking of his last time working in London, working on a prototype fusion reactor that eventually went nowhere because the UK Government got scared and canned the project not wanting to risk having something good built on UK soil, he remembers the one person he got on with or at least tolerated, John Cooper, a nuclear physicist. Looking through his contacts and finding his number, unless he's changed it but that's doubtful, he sends a text to see if he's still in London and wants a catch up, not expecting a reply, he goes straight back to his mixed grill not realising how hungry he was. Finishing his food just as his phone pings, a quick reply from John to say he's on his way, which is a surprise having convinced himself that he'd want nothing to do with him, they tolerated each other at work, but had very different ideas on subjects, John always being overly cautious and Alex taking too many risks led to plenty of heated arguments and debates between them, emptying research space of anyone else, partly because no one knew how far the arguments would go and probably didn't want to be witness to a murder, but in the end they always made up and got on in the end.

Half an hour later John comes walking through the door, with Alex waving like he's a 5-year-old at a party, the only thing missing is the party hat, John puts his hand up to acknowledge he's seen him, probably in some hope that he'll put his arm back down and stop looking like an idiot. Walking over with two drinks John sits down and the two exchange welcomes "Alex I wouldn't have expected you to contact me" Alex just laughs "Come on we weren't that bad were we?" catching up on recent events over a few more drinks, John offering his condolences when he hears about his parents, sitting talking more like friends for once since they don't have to put up with each other at work, neither of them realise that it's getting close to 8pm and they've both drank quite a bit, the two get up to leave, John is at work in the morning and Alex has some keys to collect in the morning and his parents apartment to have a look around.

Walking outside John hails a cab and offers to drop Alex off at his hotel on the way, deciding it's probably easier if jumps in the cab and about 10 minutes makes it to his hotel room and heads straight for bed, having a drank enough to send him off to sleep pretty quickly, he doesn't know anything until his alarm goes off Tuesday morning. Getting up and throwing the same clothes on he makes a coffee and packs his bag deciding he may as well stay at the apartment once he has the keys. Double checking, he has everything and finishing his coffee, he grabs his bag and makes his way down to reception checking out walking straight out, taking the walk back to the solicitor's office.

As soon as he walks in Dorothy stands up straight away, all be it a little slow, probably through fear that her back might break, she simply shows him through to Mr. Rosenthal's office, who is waiting with another pile of papers for him to sign and a set of keys in front of him. "Alex your earlier than I expected we just have a few papers to sign and the keys are yours the finances will be arranged and should be complete by the end of the day" Quickly signing everything and taking the keys Alex is out of the office half an hour later, every time he goes in there, he feels like a time traveller gone back to some bygone era. Looking at the slip of paper that his address for the apartment written on it, he hails a taxi and asks for Tower Bridge Wharf. Arriving outside the building he just stands looking, this is something he could never have afforded. Going through the doors and heading for the elevator punching the button for the penthouse apartment, the lift door opens again and he walks in, his hand shaking a little trying to get the key in the lock. As soon as he walks in, he stops, dropping his bag on the floor. The whole apartment looks like a fancy museum, glass display cases almost randomly positioned throughout the large open plan kitchen/living room, a door to the right leading to a very lavish bathroom with a jacuzzi and gold taps and a single door further down to the right leading to a huge bedroom, the front of the apartment overlooking the Thames is a wall of glass sliding doors which must be amazing during the summer. Still not moving, not even sure what he should do he just stands for a few minutes before finally gaining some composure and starts walking through the room, stopping at the display cases having a look in each one, all of them seem dedicated to explorations, one is full of artefacts from Egypt, another from Greece, then a strange display case, in the middle of the floor, the only one with no lights standing away from everything else, he saw it in the photo, that looked out of place, but actually looking at it that's different. Looking into the case at a solid piece of black rock, almost like a mirror, but not. It feels different, which doesn't seem right, how can he feel something he's not even touching. After looking at it from every angle he decides to go and sit, hanging his jacket on a chair and looking in the fridge on the way, thankfully finding a few cans of beer still in there. Walking over to the huge curved sofa with his can and sitting down, instantly drawn to the windows and the view outside, he takes a drink and puts his can down on the glass table, noticing an envelope on the table with his name neatly written on the front. Reaching for it staring at his name across the front, not sure what to think, why would this be here? Not realising he's been holding the envelope in his hands for 10 minutes, his hands sweating, he snaps out of his daze and finally decides to open it.

Alex,

We have left a letter every time we have gone on a new expedition just in case for some reason we couldn't return, usually to say how sorry we are, but this one is different. We left for Peru on Wednesday 15th July to see if we could find some undiscovered ruins. We know we have made a lot of mistakes and have never really been there for you and we regret that every day but we weren't sure that you would want any contact with us after so long and so many mistakes and missed opportunities. We have left journals for all of our expeditions in a cupboard in the bedroom for you to look at if you wish. There is an artefact that despite countless research attempts we have never been able to understand, the piece of black rock in a display case, we believe this will answer many questions about human existence and maybe human future. The only thing we have found is that it reacts to power, that is why we have it on its own away from a power source. We found it on a trip to Cortez, Colorado, your mum saw it wedged into the wall of a well at some ruins and although we shouldn't have, we took it away with us, something almost primal took over and we couldn't leave it. Be careful if you decide to try to understand it, it drains anything with power that it gets close to, everything else in the Colorado journal. Finally, one last thing please know that we love you and we have always been proud of everything you have achieved.

Mum & Dad

Sitting staring at the letter with a mix of emotions, anger, resentment and loss. Thankfully he's alone, not being a person that openly shows emotion. Now comes the question of the rock, the one thing his parents did know was that given any sort of challenge Alex is like a dog with a bone and where his parents are concerned, he'll do it anyway probably for some need of approval. Pulling out a notepad he starts trying to work out what direction to go in, does he stay in London? The apartment is a lot nicer than his dimly lit flat in Edinburgh and the weather is a little better, there's nothing in his Edinburgh flat that he's really worried about, the few things he does need to keep he usually has in his bag anyway, so that's an easy decision for him but he'll deal with the flat in due time. For now, what to do about the rock? He was already intrigued, just by its odd positioning and lack of power around it, after the reading the letter that part makes a little more sense but at the same time brings up a million questions about it. Putting the letter back in its envelope he stands up to have a closer look, making sure to leave his phone on the table remembering his parent's message about the rock reacting to power.

Standing in front of the display cabinet looking at the rock still in its glass cocoon, he can't help but get mesmerized by it, perfectly smooth almost like glass, a darkness to it that sucks you in, yet he can see his reflection like a mirror, the whole thing looks like one big contradiction. Thinking about what to do next without blinking or turning his gaze away from the rock, he snaps out of his trance and starts walking toward to the bedroom and the cupboard full of journals, he's already too invested to walk away as the chorus to Highway to Hell pops into his head on the walk through. Reaching the cupboard and looking in with a look of shock, he knew his parents liked to travel but the cupboard is full of journals and boxes, all neatly labelled on shelves for ease of use. It doesn't take long for him to spot the one marked Sedona, Arizona, taking the journal out and not seeing any boxes marked Sedona, he walks back through to the lounge with the journal tucked under one arm, not able to avoid looking at the rock on the way through. It has him and he has it.

Sitting with music playing on the Bluetooth speaker next to the TV, he starts looking through the journal, one of the main points seems to Cliff Palace, an area of ruins from an ancient settlement, again and again references to it are everywhere, so if he is going to explore the rocks origins that looks like as good a starting point as any, but first he wants to investigate the rock itself a little closer, see if he can find anything online about it or anything like it and maybe check it's relation to power. If he's going to do this, he's going to need supplies, mainly drink and snacks, maybe a nice whisky and some beer and anything he doesn't need to cook or wait for. Putting the journal down and picking his jacket up he heads out of the apartment straight to the lift, there's a supermarket nearby which doesn't take him long to get to, grabbing a basket and throwing crisps and cold snacks in, then the all-important case of beer and a bottle of whisky as he gets to the checkout. Arriving back at the apartment 20 minutes later, he throws his jacket over a kitchen chair, which then slides to the floor, takes a can from the case and puts the rest in the fridge, he goes straight back to the journal picking his laptop up on the way and sits at the table looking out over the Thames, ignoring the journal for a start and searching for Cliff Palace expecting something small, a little settlement of some sort, but he ends up more shocked at the scale of ruins.

Looking closely at the photo he starts looking through the journal, mainly the pages that involve the ruins and sees a crudely drawn picture of the site, with a red circle around the round building to the left of the ruins and an arrow with "Well" written pointing to the building, is there a well inside? Looking through the journal a little more it looks like his parents removed the black rock from the wall of the well, so if he's going to do this at least he knows where to start. Still unable to take his mind away from the rock, which almost seems to have a hold on him now, almost like it's calling him over to the cabinet, getting up and walking back over forgetting to leave his phone behind, he stands looking at the rock as it starts to slowly lift only about a centimetre but it definitely moved, then just as it looks like it's turning his phone beeps and turns off and the rock drops, shattering three glass shelves. Stunned he pulls out his phone, completely drained within seconds, then opening up the cabinet confused about how it could crash through all three shelves from such a small height, he bends to pick it up, looking at its size it shouldn't weigh much, maybe a kilogram but it takes him two hands to lift it, after that he decides it might be better just sat on the floor at the bottom of the cabinet and walks away, fetching a phone charger on the way back to the sofa.

Sitting back down scratching his head, every time he looks at that thing, he walks away with more questions than answers. Looking back at the information he found on his laptop, the site was a settlement for Anasazi which roughly translates to "The Ancient Ones", the Anasazi were native Navajo and date back to around 1000BC but the Anasazi abandoned their settlements around 1000 years ago. Sitting back and having a drink, scratching his head, trying to work out what to do next, the only thing that seems to make any sense would be a trip to Arizona, a holiday might be nice anyway, before he goes back to work.

Realising he hasn't bothered showering since leaving Edinburgh, he finishes his can off and walks to the bathroom staring down at the rock on the way past, hoping that a shower will clear his thoughts a little so that he can attempt to work out what to do next, although he already has his mind set on a holiday to Arizona. Finishing his shower and getting some clean clothes on, he starts feeling a little more human, getting another can from the fridge he sits back down and starts looking for flights, wanting to at least go and have a look at what his parents were doing there. Booking a one-way flight for now, having a working visa for the states following his time with NASA he doesn't need to worry too much about rushing back. Making sure he booked first class, wanting some comfort, it's an 11-hour flight to Tucson, so he at least wants to be comfortable, flight booked he books a night at the airport hotel. Picking up a glass and the bottle of whisky, he sits on the sofa, puts a film on and sits back to relax for a bit, having two days before his flight he hasn't planned much and not really wanting to go clothes shopping in London just yet he starts looking through Amazon for a few items to take with him, then he can go shopping in America.

    Sitting with his drink in hand he drops it in his lap falling asleep, he jumps up not realising it's almost 11pm with whiskey down his trousers, making him think he's pissed himself. He hasn't really stopped over the last few days, so he decides on climbing into bed and not setting alarms for the morning, that is until he walks into the bedroom and starts to get a weird feeling about sleeping in his dead parents bed, turning round and walking out of the bedroom with a blanket that was folded on a chair and a pillow he gets himself comfortable on the sofa it's only two nights and then he'll be on the plane anyway and he can buy a bed when he returns, having decided he wants to stay in London, at least for a bit. Comfortable enough he puts his can on the table and falls asleep pretty much straight away.

Waking a little before noon on Wednesday and wanting to wait in for his delivery to arrive, he starts gathering a few bits he'll need, the journal and a few clothes and then anything he ordered for delivery. As soon as the delivery has been he leaves straight away to go for a walk and stop for some food, not having anything to do and limited research until he gets to America, that's pretty much how Wednesday and Thursday go, with his flight at 3am Friday morning he gets a few extra hours sleep Thursday afternoon just to see him through, he can catch up on sleep on the flight.

CHAPTER 3

As Thursday slowly goes past, he's already checked his bag four times, things always take longer when you're waiting. Finally, just before midnight his taxi arrives to take him through to the airport and his trip can start, now that he's had a couple of days to rest, he's starting to look forward to a new challenge, something that at least in some way will bring him closer to his parents, as he starts to realise this is as much about understanding his parents as it is about the rock itself. Arriving at the airport just after 1am, he's got a couple of hours to make his way through the airport for his flight at 3am, security and everything on the way through doesn't take as long as he expected but he's still not used to travelling under covid restrictions, it took him longer to prove he was vaccinated than it did to get through security. Making it through to the airport lounge, he finds a seat away from everyone else, partly covid.

Sitting thinking about what he wants to do when he arrives in Tucson, a night at the airport hotel when he arrives then make his way through to Cortez the day after, meaning at least he can have a drink before the journey to Cortez. The trip itself is over 450 miles from Tucson to Cortez, but this was the easiest flight he saw at the time so he sits looking on his phone trying to find a private charter for that part of his trip, finding one company he bookmarks the site so he can arrange a flight when he gets to the hotel.

Having sat waiting for what seems like hours the call goes out for boarding and he jumps up, more than ready to get onto the plane, acting more like a kid in a sweety shop, than a grown man going on a research trip. Standing near the front of the queue it doesn't take long for him to board the plane and find his nice first-class seat, with plenty of room to spread out and of course the window, hoping to see a storm on the way, he's always had a thing about watching the lightning from above the clouds. Almost bang on 3am the pilot comes over the P.A. to announce that the plane is leaving and it starts moving into position on the runway, with Alex sat back in his seat watching out of the window lost in his own thoughts until the seat belt light goes off and the hostess's start making their way through the plane, with Alex watching intently, thinking about a whisky, it's a long flight he may as well be comfortable and enjoy it. 10 minutes later he's happily sitting with his whisky flicking through films to find something to watch, always being a Marvel geek he stops immediately on Thor: Ragnarök, puts his headphones in and reclines his seat, just enough so he's comfortable but can still see out of the window, laying back enjoying his drink and film, he doesn't realise he'd drifted off to sleep until one the hostess's walk by to see if he would like breakfast, checking his watch it's 8am UK time, 6 hours to go. As his breakfast appears he decides on switching to the radio and pulls out his phone to start looking at what exactly is in Tucson, since he's never been there, slowly eating his breakfast and scanning through google maps with little interest in anything he sees to do when he gets there, he'll probably just go for a drink and some food and build up energy for Cortez, which by the looks of it is pretty much one street through the centre, with all the shops and food places, so he starts looking for a nice place to stay since he's always had a habit of picking somewhere when he reaches his destination. Looking through google maps and checking driving times, he realises it's only a 32-mile drive from Cortez to the Cliff Palace, so Cortez will be his destination. Deciding on the Best Western in Cortez, that's one decision out of the way. Deciding just to book a night at the Best Western at Tucson airport for ease it means that when he lands, he can relax for the day, ready for Cortez.

Breakfast finished, hotel booked and finally

the announcement comes to say they will be landing shortly, Alex is almost upset that there was no turbulence or anything for the entire flight, but at least he's here now. It doesn't take long before they pull up and start departing the plane. The walk-through security didn't take long despite having to prove he's been vaccinated again and he makes his way through the airport toward the hotel, realising it's almost as quiet here as it was in London which he likes. Arriving at reception being partly amazed at the fact that a 2-star hotel in the UK, looks like you'd expect a 2-star hotel, this place looks closer to a 4-star hotel, the differences between the UK and the US always seem so big. Checking in and making it straight to his room, a little jet lagged but not too bad for having some sleep on the flight, he changes the time on his watch, just past 7am, so he decides he may as well get a little more sleep before he goes wandering.

Waking up at 11am to his alarm, he goes for a quick shower before he leaves to have a look around, trying to get back into his normal routine, having lost track of things since he left Edinburgh for London. Finding some clean clothes in his case and skipping the instant coffee in his room, he goes straight down to the hotel bar for a latte before he goes for a walk. Sitting enjoying a half decent coffee he looks at what he has around him, only seeing Pizza Hut nearby, but he's spotted a place called Cattletown Steakhouse & Saloon further into Tucson that seems more like his sort of place, once he's there he can sit and try to arrange a flight for Saturday to get to Cortez, not wanting his first drive in years being a 450-mile trip in a foreign country. Leaving the hotel deciding his destination is too much of a walk he jumps in a waiting taxi heading straight for the Steakhouse with the driver asking the usual tourist aimed questions, what brings you here? How long are you here? Where did you come from? Trying to be a pleasant as he can he answers the string of questions, thankfully the journey only takes about 10 minutes, then he realises he has no cash and has to run to the nearest ATM and take some money out to pay the driver, luckily, it's America and there seems to be an ATM every other building. Looking around, most of the buildings look like the wild west, which his inner child loves, heading straight for the steakhouse, a fairly old-fashioned sort of place that fits in almost perfectly with the look of the outside of the building, first things first a drink, then sort out travel to Cortez. After that he can relax for the day.

Finding a quiet corner, he pulls up the site for a private charter to Cortez, with everything being quiet at the moment it doesn't take long to phone them and arrange the flight, with the guy on the phone seeming almost too happy for some business, his flight is planned for 12pm Sunday, meaning he doesn't have to rush in the morning and he can try to get his body clock in order before he starts his research properly. Sitting back and enjoying his beer, his mind starts wandering back to the rock, but there is nothing that would explain its properties or what the Anasazi would use it for, the closest eruption he's been able to find anything about was millions of years ago, could the rock have been there for that long? And if so, how? The rock itself doesn't look like any obsidian he's ever seen and the weight of the rock doesn't match up, if it is obsidian, it shouldn't weigh anywhere near as much as it does and why does it need power?, it's not like the Anasazi were on the grid. The other problem with finding what the rock is made of without letting anybody else handle it, feeling safer keeping this to himself at least for now, he decides to pass on that idea. Looking back at google maps to see what else is around and not seeing anything interesting he orders a steak and a couple of drinks, wanting something to eat before he heads back to the hotel, then probably go and sit in the bar for a bit to waste a little time. Eating his steak, he almost seems sorry he needs to leave Tucson, he could quite happily come back here every day for dinner, but he has things to do, he'll just have to hope he can get a good steak in Cortez. Finishing his steak and drinks he leaves a nice tip and walks back out to look for a taxi, after getting some more cash from the ATM, checking his balance before he takes any money out, he almost faints, the money has been transferred into his account, he didn't receive any emails or anything to tell him it had been completed but his balance is now showing over £15million in his account, snapping out of his shock with the ATM beeping asking him if he wants to continue he takes out $200 to last him a few days and hails a taxi and sits quietly looking at the receipt from the ATM. Arriving back at the hotel without saying a word on the taxi ride back he heads straight for the bar needing something to settle him down again, trying to hand money over with his hand shaking. He stays in the bar till the evening before heading up to his room to put a film on and get some sleep before his flight the next day. Back in his room he crawls straight into bed setting an alarm for 8am and falls asleep almost straight away, only to be woken by a nightmare about his parents, then taking another hour to drift off again.

CHAPTER 4

Jumping awake when his alarm goes off in the morning, he gets out of bed and instantly makes a coffee needing something to combat the jet lag before he leaves. Taking a drink and almost spitting it out when he realises how bad hotel coffee is, he pours the coffee away he and quickly packs his bag and makes his way down to reception wanting to check out and have a semi decent coffee before he leaves for a private airport, the taxi was arranged by the charter company for 10am giving him an hour to have a couple of cups of coffee before he leaves, he never usually has much of an issue with jet lag, but this time round it's hit him like a bus. After his second latte he heads outside for a bit of fresh air, 5 minutes later his taxi pulls, thankfully the driver knows where he needs to go, because it dawned on Alex just as he climbed into the taxi, he has no idea where he's going. Watching contently out of the window as they drive through Tucson leaving the buildings behind and heading into open fields and farm's he spots a small plane sat on a runway a couple of fields down, hoping that that's his plane, now that he's had a little time, he's looking forward to being able to sink his teeth into researching what exactly his parents were doing and what that rock is.

Pulling straight in and driving through a hangar that's open both ends, the taxi stops right next to small set of steps leading into the plane, pilot standing ready to greet him, even for the amount of travelling he's done for work this is a new one for Alex. Exchanging names and greetings with the pilot he's shown on to the plane, which is a lot nicer inside than it looked from the outside, four seats two on one side facing each other with a table between them and the same on the other side, with a small chiller under both tables that the pilot has already stocked for him. Getting seated on a nice comfy leather recliner that looks like it should be in a CEO's office rather than a plane, he leans down to the chiller and grabs a can of beer, then sits back and slips the seatbelt on as the pilot asks if he's ready? Still looking at the interior of the plane, which reminds him of Tony Starks private jet, minus the champagne, which is no bad thing, it's just wine with added bubbles and wine doesn't exactly agree with Alex, something he learnt a long time ago, after waking up in a bush covered in sick when he was in his early 20's.

As the plane starts moving down the runway, he starts to realise how stunning the landscape is out here, fields of different colours, broken only by the occasion field of animals. The flight shouldn't take long, about three hours and then his taxi from the airport to his hotel, the Best Western in Cortez has already been arranged by the charter company for when they land. Watching out of the window drinking a beer time passes a little quicker, quietly thinking about how to start when he's settled in Cortez, does he hire a car or get taxis? He hasn't driven for a while, living in cities he never really saw the point, most of the time the roads were either closed for roadworks or backed up with traffic, so he never bothered and has never owned a car. Then there's the question of where does he start his research? Probably Cliff Palace, or at least that seems like the most logical place to start, at the source, where the rock was taken from, which for now at least is safely sitting on the floor of his parent's apartment surrounded by glass that he probably should have tidied up before he left. The pilot tells him they will be descending soon, not realising time had passed so quickly he slides the seatbelt back on and puts his chair upright again as the plane starts heading back down to solid land. Landing without any issue he sees his taxi driving toward the plane and pulling up by the ladder as the pilot walks round and opens the door, thanking the pilot Alex climbs down and jumps straight into his waiting taxi and they drive off towards Cortez and his hotel, he was in such a daydream on the flight that he didn't realise just how immense the Mesa Verde National

Park really is, over 52000 acres of protected land and several old ruins and sightseeing spots await him.

As the taxi pulls out Alex drops into his daydream again, having never really been in areas of the States like this, it's all new and a lot nicer than the big cities he's seen in the past, more farmland and glimpses of Mesa Verde on the way through to Cortez. As they start the drive into Cortez itself it reminds him a little of Tucson, older looking buildings, somewhere in between wild west and those postcard towns you never really believe exist until you're in one and all surrounded by open land and hills. The drive through Cortez doesn't take long and soon they arrive at his hotel on the main street in Cortez, paying the driver and stepping out of the taxi, he takes a deep breath and stretches looking around the large car park. Walking through the doors into a reception that looks surprisingly lavish compared to the almost motel looking layout of the rooms. The woman behind the desk is nice and polite, probably glad to see another human since covid has almost wiped-out visitor numbers around most of the globe, a small smile as she hands his key card over and points him in the direction of his room. Taking a slow walk out of reception and round to his room, enjoying the sun which is nice after a pretty miserable winter in Scotland. Sliding his card into the lock he walks in to a room that makes his flat in

Edinburgh look like it was taken over by squatters, a nice king size bed, desk, TV and a jacuzzi style bath in a nice and clean hotel room will at least make his stay comfortable. Looking out of the window at the back of the room, which looks out to a swimming pool outside, that will go along nicely with the indoor pool he saw on the hotels website before he booked. The only downside he can think of is the lack of a bar, but there's plenty of places local he can go for a drink and food if he wants. Putting his bag in the wardrobe, taking out his laptop and placing it on the desk he sits down, tired from all the travelling but not wanting to sleep yet, mainly because he wants to try and clear the jet lag as soon as possible.

Opening up his laptop he starts looking for places nearby to go for a drink and some food and try to decide what he wants to do, for starters working out how far the cliff palace is from his hotel and how he's going to travel, does he want to finally cave and hire a car or rely on taxi's? Quickly looking at directions he decides he'll probably be better hiring a car, but all of that can wait till he's had food, drink and sleep. Picking up his wallet and phone he heads out to go and find somewhere nice to eat and relax, leaving his room and walking straight back out into the January sun of Cortez he walks over to the hotel reception, wondering if he can find any information that might help him with his research. Talking to the receptionist, she hands him a number of a local native American guide called Achak who might be able to help and a handful of tourist leaflets, sliding the card into his phone case he walks back and takes a slow walk round to a Mexican restaurant he spotted on google maps, looking around him as he walks down East Main Street, the whole town looks like something from a western movie, besides of course the modern signs for places like Pizza Hut and McDonalds. Walking past a burger drive-in and a couple of other places he reaches the door for La Casita De Cortez, a place that looks like it would fit into one of the Back to The Future films, the one where they went back to the wild west. As soon as he walks in, he's greeted by a young female waitress called Inez, it's early in the day still so apart from a couple of older men sitting at the bar he's the only there, he gets seated at the window and picks up the menu, his eyes instantly spot the nachos and the drinks, nachos, light beer and a nice bourbon would go down nicely right now. It doesn't take long before he's ordered and has his drinks, sitting looking out of the window his mind starts to wander back to the rock and his real purpose for being here, though a holiday at the same time is a nice idea. He can see the rock easily in his mind, a black piece of rock, that would normally be quite unassuming, but there is something strange, something he can't put his finger on, a certain pull, then of course there's the relation to power, what the hell is that? He's always been interested in sci-fi films and programmes and at the moment it's hard not to think about a more outrageous angle for the rock. Just as his nachos arrive, he slips the card back out of his phone case and decides to call him now, thankful that he has roaming on his network because one thing he didn't do was check that before he left the UK.

It takes two rings for Achak to answer in an obvious native American accent, Alex instantly jumps straight in and asks him about the Cliff Palace, after a short chat and Achak telling him pretty much everything he already knew they arrange for Achak to pick him up in the morning at the hotel and drive over to show him around and tell him more of the history of the site, which is just what Alex wants, he can't help but think that there is something strange about the Anasazi, for a start it appears they had established a strong settlement in the area but then they vanished 1000 years ago for no obvious reason, but he can ask Achak about all of that tomorrow.

For now, he can relax and enjoy his nachos and drinks, maybe go for a walk around town and see what Cortez is like and find a nice coffee shop. It doesn't take long for him to finish up realising he was hungrier than he thought, walking back out into the sun and taking a look around he starts a steady walk toward the veteran's park, remembering he saw a welcome centre nearby, guessing it's kind of like a tourist information centre, he might be able to pick up some more leaflets and maybe a map, not so much for research more for something he can use to track where he's been and any areas of interest he might need to revisit. Walking along the road he's still amazed at the look of all the buildings, ideas of running down the street, galloping like a horse screaming Yee-haw go through his head, but he keeps the laugh and the idea internal, not really thinking it would go down well with the locals. Walking past the liquor store he makes a mental note of it for later and on the opposite side Garcia & Co. jewellers, the buildings along East Main Street all seem quite spread out rather than being wall to wall making the place look bigger than it really is. Walking past the hotel he's staying at which remarkably nice and modern compared to the rest of the area, the parking lot is spotless, the building itself is a lot cleaner, especially compared to the small hut down the road, the GDP HQ, with its outside covered in flags and banners, fighting for votes. Carrying on down the road he can't help but laugh at a sign outside another liquor store "Beer is now cheaper than gas Drink Don't Drive" sound advice if he does say so himself, finally making it to the Colorado Welcome Centre he pushes the door open and steps in, racks of leaflets line the walls, an old woman sat behind the desk with librarian glasses on, he starts looking through leaflets and finds half a dozen that might be useful, then walks over to the desk to ask if they have maps. Without cracking a smile or more to the point without any emotion at all and not a word the old woman hands him a map and goes back to the crossword she's sat trying to think of answers for, thinking to himself yay welcome to Colorado please don't enjoy your stay, heading back to the hotel, thinking of sitting out by the pool with his map, leaflets and laptop and trying to do some more focused research now he's here and feeling a little fuller of energy now. 9am in the morning he's being picked up by Achak to go and look at the ruins and hopefully find some answers while he's there.

Arriving back at the hotel 10 minutes later and sat out by the pool with everything he needs another 5 minutes later, he starts scanning the map looking for the cliff palace overlook, tomorrow's destination. Finding it and drawing a big red circle around it he puts his coffee on the map to hold it in place, not fancying chasing it around the pool if that breeze picks it up. Shuffling through the leaflets he picked up and finding one for the four corners area, a monument to mark where Arizona, Colorado, New Mexico, and Utah meet, it also marks the point the boundary between two semi-autonomous native American governments, the Navajo and the Ute, which may be important at some point, so he marks another circle on the map. The next leaflet he finds is about the Anasazi, a name he's getting used to seeing now, almost all of their history is based around the four corners area, with several different interpretations of their name, the ancient ones, ancestral Pueblo culture amongst the many different ones he's seen, but he's taken a liking to the ancient ones, sounds more adventurous to him. Looking through the leaflet, he sees the same bit that he's always found strange, the culture dates back around 2000 years and seem to vanish after around 1000 years although descendants still carry on many of their customs and traditions, the settlements themselves were left, almost in a hurry with pottery and other artefacts just left for archaeologists to find hundreds of years later, a lot of people looked to the Spaniards who were very busy in the area, mainly searching for and looting gold from native tribes and civilisations but eventually that was all but disregarded when it came to the Anasazi. The trail seems to have gone pretty cold on why they left and where they went, with almost nothing being found apart from what was left behind, skeletal remains, trinkets and artefacts. There was very little written history to make things harder for researchers, the only written history came from the Spaniards the rest was pictographs left around their sites, which are always open to interpretation, especially if you watch ancient aliens.

Putting his leaflets in a neat pile and folding the map and placing it all on the table underneath his laptop to save them blowing away, he leans back in his chair and takes a drink. Looking at his watch he didn't realise he'd been reading leaflets and planning where he needs to go for about four hours and is starting to get hungry again, he remembered a Pizza Hut just up from the hotel and puts everything in his room and heads back out for food, then probably an early night ready for tomorrow. Walking down the road as it starts to cool outside, he walks into Pizza Hut and quickly orders a Pizza and a drink, starting to feel tired again, all he can think of is getting back to his room and climbing into bed, which is exactly what he does, the minute his head hits the pillow he's out cold until his alarm goes off at 7am ready for his first part of his research.

CHAPTER 5

Waking up to his alarm Tuesday morning the only thing he can think about is coffee and what he might or might not find on his trip to the cliff palace. Sitting at the desk in his room sipping his coffee he starts thinking about his story not wanting to make any reference to his parents being connected to a piece of rock that was taken from the site, he has no idea if anyone even knows about it or not. Finishing his coffee, he still has an hour before his guide turns up, so he gets ready and makes his way to the dining room for some breakfast, a little fuel for his day ahead, walking out of his room to a cool January morning but still probably about 5 degrees warmer than Edinburgh or London, heading straight for the hotel reception, not really paying attention to the receptionist he walks straight through to the dining room to the smell of bacon and coffee, the perfect mix for 8am. Making a bee line for the hot breakfast, 2 strips of bacon, eggs, beans and sausage, the bacon is obviously coated in something sweet it always seems to be in America, but bacon is bacon no matter what they do to it, getting another coffee he sits by the window looking out to the parking lot for his guide turning up. Shovelling his breakfast down not wanting to leave anything on his plate when he has to leave, he pushes his plate away, pleasantly full and drinks his coffee as a black Mercedes pulls in and parks almost directly in front of the window he's sitting at, a tall man with obvious native American appearance and clothing, he fits perfectly in Cortez with its wild west feel. Watching him through the window walking past toward the reception Alex finishes his coffee and stands up as Achak walks through the door. Introducing themselves the two shake hands and head out to the black Mercedes ready for their road trip.

As they pull out of the car park Achak starts asking what brings him to Cortez? Making his excuses not mentioning his parents, he tells him what he can without lying, mentioning several documentaries he's seen and wanting to see for himself, which seems to go down well with Achak. Through most of the hour drive Achak explains his roots, being a descendant of the Anasazi people and talking about the culture which Alex finds surprisingly interesting. Leaving Cortez along Highway 160 the buildings end abruptly to show open land with very few buildings and stunning landscapes. As they enter the Mesa Verde national park the landscape turns to a rockier and hillier than the landscape they've left behind and much more amazing. Alex sits happily looking out of the window watching as they pass, seeing the odd signs of ruins from past cultures most of them probably related to the Anasazi, but the one he's interested in the most right now is the cliff palace sight and maybe some of the others depending on what he finds.

Arriving at the car park nearest the cliff palace both men get out of the car and Achak starts walking round toward the path leading to the site with Alex closely following. As they follow the bend round nothing could have prepared Alex for what he saw, the photos looked amazing on their own, but the site he saw was stunning, the ruins look so well developed that he can't help but realise that the Anasazi were more advanced than he gave them credit for. Talking to Achak asking about their cultural and religious beliefs, Achak starts explaining about the many petroglyphs around the mesa Verde area, most seem to revolve around animals, which were highly prized by the Anasazi, but almost images of people or beings that appear far too tall to be from around here, different theories relate to these images, from other cultures belief in the "star people" extra-terrestrial beings that aided the advancement of cultures and the occasional mention of giants which Achak promptly laughs away seemingly more inclined to believe in aliens rather than giants. Looking from the railings surrounded the site is amazing but

Alex wants to get closer, whether he can or not is a different matter, but he tries his luck and asks Achak who very quickly refuses, mentioning briefly some tourists that removed a highly prized artefact from the site around a year ago. Quickly leaving that conversation behind Alex asks if they could see some of the petroglyphs, which thankfully makes Achak smile and start leading him round to the closest ones, Alex hadn't realised how long they had been here, they left the hotel at 9am and now it's getting close to 4pm. As they turn another bend in the path it leads them to a smooth rock wall covered in drawings carved into its face. Alex steps closer taking photos on his phone probably close to a hundred now since they arrived here, looking at the details he starts to see what Achak was talking about, the tall slim beings that look too different to simply be normal people and on all of the images they have their arms raised to the sky, apart from those there are a lot of drawings of normal sized beings more likely to be human and animals and a lot of swirls and strange shapes. Whatever story they were trying to tell in these images goes straight over Alex's head, he turns to Achak to ask what he thinks, Achak simply answers "It's open to interpretation even within my culture we all believe different things, we take from it what we choose to believe" At that Achak signals for them to start the walk back to his car, seemingly not wanting to around here when the sun starts to get low, which Alex doesn't question, he's already formulating a plan of his own, he doesn't need Achak to be here for that part.

Arriving back at the black Mercedes Achak starts the drive back, with Alex quite happily asking questions about the culture and mainly why they left their settlements, which Achak explains that again there are many theories but nothing solid to explain it, they appeared 2000 years ago and seemed to vanish 1000 years later, but no one seems to know where they came from or where they went to, which makes Alex start wondering about the rock again. Could the rock really be something he hasn't considered yet? Even for Alex when he's thinking more from his love his Sci-Fi would find that hard to believe, but why were his parents so interested in that rock? Out of everything in their apartment why only the rock? Why do they want him to look into that and nothing else?

Not realising he'd stopped talking about halfway back, as they pull into the hotel parking lot, he makes his excuses and says he's tired and thanks Achak for his time and all of the information he gained from the trip and heads back toward his room to get changed before he heads out for some food and a drink. Charging his phone for ten minutes while he gets changed so that he can sit and look through the photos from his trip to cliff palace while he eats, he quickly throws on some clean clothes, picks up a notepad and puts his phone back in his pocket and heads straight back out to look for food deciding on some Thai food this time he turns right out the hotel and heads down the road to Thai Cortez & Sushi, dismissing the idea of raw fish immediately but a green curry would go down well with a few drinks. Arriving at the restaurant, which looks like a wild west Chinese takeaway, if there was such a thing, walking in to a spotless white tiled floor and wooden tables, he's seated by an older man and asks for a beer while he looks at the menu, which is almost pointless since he had already decided what he wanted before he arrived, his drink arrives and he immediately orders a Thai green curry.

While he waits for his food he sits drinking his beer and flicking through photos from the day, especially the one he got of the well, zoomed and crystal clear he can see exactly where his parents found the rock, but the rock just doesn't seem to fit anything he saw while he was at the site, all the buildings are the same colour, not one spot of black anywhere and no mention of any other artefacts, but he was wise not to mention his parents since Achak did mention some tourists that removed an artefact from the site, he dodged that bullet well. Just as his food turns up his mind starts thinking about the plan moving forward, trying to decide on whether to hire a car or not, there's a lot of places he'd like to look at and he doesn't really want to draw attention to himself by constantly asking Achak to take him and he has an idea of going back to the cliff palace at night, alone to see if he can get closer. Talk of star people and some things he's seen in documentaries pop into his mind, although he finds these things hard to believe outside of wild theories and cheap sci-fi films, he has this feeling that he needs to see for himself while he's here.

Finishing his food, he decides on a trip to the coffee shop near the hotel to get a decent takeaway coffee and head back to his room and search for a hire car company for the next day so that he can go where he wants without interruptions. Making it back to his room, he starts to realise just how tired he actually is and checks the time almost 11pm, his thoughts had been so focused on what he's doing he hadn't even noticed it getting dark outside. The hire car can wait till tomorrow for now he'll find a film lay on the bed and have a drink, not finding much to watch he ends up putting Independence Day on, which after the day of walking around the ruins makes him laugh, thinking of aliens in Sedona

CHAPTER 6

After a better sleep and feeling a little more refreshed he makes his usual morning coffee and sits at the desk with his laptop looking at hire cars, the question is, with his extra wealth does he go all out and hire something expensive or stick with something small and more kitted out for the drives he'll be doing? Deciding on something sensible for now, considering it's been a while since he's driven anything, he doesn't really fancy wrapping a Ferrari around a lamp post. Finding a hire company nearby and arranging the hire easily enough, he sits and finishes his coffee, pulling the map out and looking at any other areas he might need to visit, another area that has been catching his eye is Square Tower House, although his parents didn't make any notes about anything other than cliff palace and the rock, he circles it anyway it's not far from cliff palace and he wants another look at the petroglyphs without anyone looking over his shoulder, he can't shake the feeling that Achak didn't exactly trust him.

Finishing his coffee just as his phone rings,

the car hire company to tell him his cars outside, almost running outside, he meets the driver hands his license and everything over for him to inspect, takes the keys and that's it, now he doesn't need anyone else, Achak was useful and knew a lot, but he also knew about his parents and that's enough he doesn't need to know that they were Alex's parents. Walking back to his room he picks up what he needs, map, phone and a couple of leaflets and heads back out swinging the car key round and round on his finger, like a cowboy who's found a car works better than a horse. Putting his seatbelt on he remembers how long it's been since he was in the driver's seat, with slightly sweaty palms and a look of complete concentration he decides before anything he'll drive around the parking lot a little, three stalls before he actually gets moving, thankfully he picks it up again fairly easily and decides to set the sat nav for the square tower house and sort some music before he sets off, slowly at first till he feels brave enough to hit the speed limit, which annoys several local drivers.

A little over an hour and a half mainly due to it being a little further round than cliff palace and driving a little slower than Achak did, he arrives at the small car park by the square tower house. Almost as amazed as he was when they pulled up at Cliff Palace, the buildings, almost look like they should be here, just a part of the landscape, then the questions start running through his head as he scribbles notes down in his notepad. Why did they build like this? You can almost see the purpose for every building in the way it's been designed. The area has a few people around it so the chance of getting any closer than the railings looking out at it right now is out of the question. Looking at his map again, there is another area of petroglyphs a short walk from where he is, so folding his map up and heading off, he starts the walk around the path to see if these are any different. When he eventually gets there, what he sees is almost the same but there is something else, the tall character in the petroglyph holding his hands to the sky seems to be almost holding something up, something that looks the same shape as the rock that is sitting back at his parents London apartment, his London apartment now, except on the petroglyph there's a line, almost like a lightning bolt going to the top of it, is that their power? Lightning? It would make sense... Can that be true? Surely not, but why not? It came from this area so why the hell wouldn't it be in a petroglyph? Has he actually found a solid link? Deciding he's got enough from this area he walks back toward the car park and takes the short drive round to Cliff Palace for another look during the day, his plan after this is to head back have a look around Cortez for a couple of days and then drive back at night to see if anything happens.

Arriving back at Cliff Palace, the areas quiet

now so he manages to get a decent vantage point, pulling his phone out he uses his camera to zoom in on the well in the centre, noting the odd bits on the way down, all the circular areas seem to be built the same, but this one is different, it looks deeper than the rest, he needs a closer look, but not in daylight, he doesn't want to be spotted, so tomorrow night he'll be back after dark, when he's alone and can stay out of sight just behind the well and see what happens. For now, he wants to get back for some food sit and have a drink and relax for the rest of the day and take it easy tomorrow before he comes back for the night. Reaching his hire car and settling into the driver's seat, he's just about to start moving when a black Mercedes comes rolling into the car park, he almost thinks about hiding, why? He has no idea, it's not like he's doing anything weird, so he just puts the car into drive and slowly rolls past Achak's car and starts the drive back to the hotel. Disturbed blasting away on the radio and the window open for a bit of fresh air, he's starting to find enjoyment in driving around this area, the landscape is amazing and the roads have almost no potholes compared to Edinburgh. Arriving back at his hotel, he parks up, goes to put the car key in his room and walks straight back out to go for a drink, it's 3pm now so he can have a relaxing day, if his mind will let him, at the moment his thoughts are spinning with ideas and thoughts about what he has already seen and what he hopes to see.

He heads straight back to La Casita De Cortez with nachos on his mind and gets seated by the window again, drinking his beer and eating nacho's, he starts to realise this could be the only thing that's actually felt like a holiday he's had for a long time and he intends to enjoy it as much as possible. He can't help but get excited about his plan for the next few days, maybe he's more like his parents than he would have liked to admit, now that he's started exploring what the rock is about, he wants to keep going and see where it leads, he may have found a new line of work, he has the money to do what he wants, so why not?

Finishing his drink and nachos and ordering another, just sitting at the window, watching the world go by, half an hour passes and he finishes his drink and pays his bill. Wanting to go to the store nearby hoping they have clothes so that he can buy some shorts, get back to the hotel put shorts on, take some beer and go and relax in the pool at the back of the hotel. Thankfully he finds a store that has some clothes and he finds a pair of shorts, getting changed quickly and grabbing a towel from the bathroom and the case of beer he heads out the back, setting his case of beer down at the side of the pool and jumps straight in struggling to catch his breath as he realises how cold the water is, this is probably the first time in years he's been able to switch off and not worry about anything for a long time.

Just as the sun starts to go down, he climbs out of the pool, dries off and sets his beer at one of the tables and goes to get changed into something a little warmer, there is very little light pollution here compared the UK, so he wants to sit out for a bit and see the stars for the first time in a long time. As the sun sets and the glow of the moon seems to be almost the only light in the sky he sits back drinking from a can as the stars start to twinkle into view and for the first time in years without a telescope he can see the milky way and he starts thinking about all the possibilities that lay waiting out there, a billion possibilities, surely we can't be alone in the universe, all those planets orbiting stars like our sun, we can't be completely alone, you'd have more chance of winning the lottery than being the only intelligent life in the universe. He starts to wonder what it would be like to meet another intelligent race, what would they think of us? Would they be more advanced? Would they want violence or peace? In his heart he would love peace and an exchange of ideas, but with how we treat each other he finds it hard to convince himself that we would be willing to treat them any better than we treat other humans. We have made many discoveries in our evolution but most end up the same way, used for violence and war. We have many different religions but they all end up fighting against each other and why? Because we can't possibly be allowed to have our own beliefs, we are a race that needs something to believe in, for Alex he wants to believe there is a better place than earth, somewhere that doesn't require weapons and war and a desperate desire for power.

Deciding around midnight that it might be time for some sleep and plan out his next few days, the main thing he wants to do is get to the ruins at Cliff Palace again, alone and at night, there is something telling him he needs to do it, some gut feeling, that and wanting to look around the ruins alone and not just from the path.

CHAPTER 7

The next day he almost jumps out of bed and starts gathering things together for his night time trip, phone and battery bank, he needs some snacks and drink to keep him going through the night, warm clothes and maybe go and get a torch so he doesn't break his neck tripping on rocks or end up falling into the well. Heading out wondering if he can get away with a couple of drinks during the day since he isn't planning to leave till about 9pm, he heads back to his favourite Mexican restaurant for some more nachos and a couple of beers before he goes shopping for the night ahead. It doesn't take him long to do what he needs to do getting back to his room a few hours later for a nap before the drive, not wanting to fall asleep during his research. Waking up about 8pm he grabs his bag which has been neatly packed and goes for a coffee in the dining room, just as he gets his coffee and sits down by the window, he looks out to see a black Mercedes parked by the car park entrance, having made a mental note of the Achak's registration plate, he knows straight away that it's him, sat in his car this time with a friend, did he attract this attention so easily? maybe his name? Right now, he doesn't care, he has his research to do, this is why his parents left this one thing with him, they know what he's like, give him a focus and he's like a dog with a bone, he won't give it up no matter how difficult it might be. The one saving grace right now is that it's dark out and as far as he knows they shouldn't be able to see him sat here with his coffee.

Just as he thinks they won't leave, he sees the headlight's come to life and they slowly pull out of the parking lot, heading in the opposite direction, which gives him some hope he won't be interrupted tonight. Feeling a little safer he finishes his coffee and heads straight to the hire car, wanting to get away quick in case they decide to return. Driving out of the parking lot himself making sure he's on the wrong side of the road, that's the only way he can remember, drive wrong and you're getting it right. Leaving East Main Street and driving down Highway 160 he starts to relax a little, following his sat-nav with Disturbed playing on the radio the drive seems a lot quicker by himself, probably because he hasn't realised, he's been over the speed limit for most of the drive. Arriving at Cliff Palace, he looks for a parking space out of the way in case Achak and his friend decide to come and check, he spots a space in the corner with a tree obscuring the view from the road and pulls in, taking his bag from the passenger seat, he locks the car and starts to walk straight down the side path leading to the access gate for the site, pausing to quickly check he's alone and quickly heads to a spot in the far corner that he'd made a note of during his first trip here, nice, secluded and out of sight.

Settling down against a rock, glad he bought a cushion from the hotel to sit, he starts getting what he needs ready, phone with a full charge, his battery bank and snacks and sits watching the stars above him. Nothing seems to be happening but there's a feeling in the air, almost like a tension, like you're walking a tight rope, fall on one side and you land on the mat below, fall on the other side and off you go down the rabbit hole, although he's starting to feel like he's already gone down the rabbit hole. Just as he starts thinking this was a waste of time the air changes from tension to charged, an electric charge that makes the hairs on his arms stand to attention and forces him to focus even more. Looking everywhere not quite sure what's going on suddenly the area becomes lighter almost like sunrise, but it's 3am and the sun won't rise for at least another 4 hours. Looking up and there it is, a bright glowing orb that seems to have appeared from nowhere, hovering gently just above the ruins.

Staring up at the orb not able to move or shift his gaze, suddenly it starts to slowly drop and for the first time he can see that it's directly above the well he'd been concentrating on. As it gets lower, he manages to get to his feet which seems almost impossible, his body doesn't want to move and it takes a lot of effort to convince it that it needs to move. Standing looking the orb is almost at eye level now, without realising he started recording a video on his phone. With the orb at eye level, he can see what looks like some sort of blue crystal in its centre, just hovering there, but there's a feeling that goes with it, like it knows something but not just something, it knows everything, it studies the world and right now it's studying Alex. The feeling leaves him feeling nervous, afraid and naked. What the hell is this? Just as he starts to think he'll be stuck staring at this until the sun rises, it drops suddenly, straight down and into the well, running over as quick as he can with his phone recording everything, he looks down the well and almost falls over. What he sees makes no sense, he's staring down a well that he saw during the day and he's seen photos of, with a dusty bottom and almost nothing else, now he stares at the bottom in complete disbelief, he's staring at the opening of a cave. Holding his phone directly over the well recording all of it, he suddenly jumps back almost losing his balance as the orb suddenly shoots directly back up and out of the well at a speed that doesn't look possible, followed by a single lightning strike straight into the well, when he gets back to the well, all he sees is the dusty rock bottom, no view of a cave, just an unassuming ruined well, not even scorched by the lightning.

Walking slowly back to his secluded corner and sitting back against the rock again, he feels like every sense has been attacked, including senses he didn't know existed. Looking at the footage on his phone, staring at the cave in the bottom of a well, that he almost convinced himself he couldn't have seen, that would be impossible right? But how can you deny it when you're looking at an image of it on your phone? Not realising the time as the sky starts to give way, from stars to the glow of a beautiful sunrise, he kneels on the floor at his bag and puts everything away, then forces himself to his feet, which feel like concrete blocks. Then suddenly he snaps out of his current state, realising he needs to get out of here before anyone turns up, he takes a quick jog back to the main path and over to his hire car. This time there is no music, no speeding, he's too distracted by what he's seen.

The drive back takes just under an hour, the roads are nice and quiet at this time of day, walking back into his room and sitting at the desk with a coffee to try and settle his nerves, he sits staring at the paused image on his phone, the image of a cave and a forest. Is this the true meaning of that glass like black rock back in London? A portal? As much as he tries to convince himself that isn't possible, the more he can't deny what he's seen. Is this why the rock needs power?

Is that what the blue crystal looking thing was in the middle of the orb? A power source? Powered by lightning? Then his mind starts to formulate a plan without him realising. He needs a power source, a powerful one, then maybe, just maybe he'll be able to use the rock to recreate what he saw down the well. But not just recreate it, but stabilise it, is that even possible?

Sitting with his head spinning he makes the decision to finally get some sleep, then when he wakes up, he needs to get a flight booked back to London and back to that rock, after one more night at Cliff Palace. He needs to work out how to power it, the whole idea seems ridiculous, but it feels right. Almost like that knowing feeling he got from the orb, like it was passing millions of years of knowledge to him to use for something, but what?

Climbing into bed and trying to quiet his mind racing mind, it doesn't seem he's going to get a good sleep and he'd be right on that part, two hours later he wakes up again, somehow with his head at the bottom of the bed, the duvet and pillows on the floor and what feels like a pulled muscle in his right arm, not exactly a restful sleep, but it's now almost lunch time and he's not planning on driving anywhere today. Getting dressed and walking out of his room into an almost blinding winter sun he starts walking back to La Casita De Cortez for some food and drink.

This time he notices something out of place just before he walks in, Achak and his mysterious friend, sat by the window. Luckily, they didn't see him and he takes the opportunity to turn around, walking past the window quickly without being spotted he heads a little further down the road to a place called Main Street Brewery & Restaurant, already day dreaming of steak and beer. Walking in and asking to be seated toward the back of the restaurant, he orders a beer and sits back, out of view of the windows he can relax a little and look at flights to get home, somehow, he knows exactly what he needs to do when he gets home and he knows exactly how to get what he needs.

CHAPTER 8

Sitting enjoying his steak and drinks looking through his phone for flights, somehow it almost feels like he's had a boost of some sort, all he can think about is the next step and the pain of having to wait till he gets back to London, but that will come soon enough. It doesn't take long to get his flight booked and rental car arranged to be picked up in 2 days' time, enough time for one more night at Cliff Palace. For now all he wants to do is pick up some cans from the liquor store, go sit by the pool and make some notes while enjoying the night sky. Finishing his food that's exactly what he plans to do and pays his bill and almost runs out of the door and to the liquor store. Walking back along the road toward the liquor store, he catches that black Mercedes out of the corner of his eye, pulling out of the hotel parking lot, driving off in the direction of the ruins, pushing it to the back of his mind not really feeling like that's his concern right now, he walks into the liquor store, picks up a case of beer and a small bottle of bourbon and walks over to pay, this time the person behind the till takes on the appearance of someone that has been drinking all the profits, reminding him of one those hillbillies you see in the movies, two front teeth like bugs bunny, shallow cheeks and dead eyes, like the spark has been snuffed out and they only operate on autopilot. Back out of the liquor store he takes the short walk back to the hotel and straight for his room, it's not as warm today so he puts a hoody on instead of his coat and picks up his laptop and notebook and heads to set himself up outside, for the first time he's realised he hasn't seen another person sat out by the pool since he's been here but he likes that, it means he can have peace away from crowds.

Heading to the bathroom before he gets settled at the table outside, he suddenly notices a white envelope sat on the floor by the door, picking it up and putting it in his pocket until he gets back outside. Out of the bathroom he walks through slipping the envelope back out of his pocket and sits down outside, tearing the envelope open he realises why the black Mercedes was pulling out of the parking lot.

Alex,

Be careful what you are doing, we know where you were overnight and some things are meant to be left alone by outsiders, there are things here you could never understand STAY AWAY FROM HERE!

Not needing the letter signed to know where it came from, he puts it in the inside cover of his notebook and leaves it there not really thinking about it, he's going home in 2 days why would he need to worry? His flights booked and he'll be away from here. Deciding on just having an easy day before he heads back to Cliff Palace and some rest before the flight home, he passes the day making notes and trying to think of a decent power source he could use. The only idea that comes to mind that might work requires more than a little black mail and a favour from an old acquaintance, but it might work. He can worry about that once he's back on UK soil and away from his new unwanted friends.

As it gets toward evening, he decides to go for a walk and a last few drinks at the Main Street Brewery before he heads to bed. Sitting by the window with a nice cold beer, he drops into almost a daydream just watching cars and people pass by, then without warning a hand lands on his shoulder, not expecting it he spins round with his fist clenched to see Achak smiling at him "Hello my friend we didn't expect to see you around tonight after the note we left you" with Alex looking around for the second person and spots him at the bar "I don't know what your issue with me is but you can fuck off I'll be back in the UK soon and you can find another tourist to stalk" Achak stands laughing as his friend comes walking over with three drinks, placing one down in front of Alex and passing another to Achak, the creepy man with the Black Mercedes finally opens his mouth "Mr Mackintosh please let me introduce myself my name is Awanyu" which in turn makes Alex burst out laughing, a full belly laugh "I'm not as uneducated as you might think, you on the other hand chose a fake name to give me, but a name that belongs to a snake god, you sure as hell got the snake part right" Awanyu stands looking insulted and a more than a little stupid "You may laugh but we know more about you than you think, we know who your parents are or should I said were, now that we hear they died in a crash, we also know that they stole an artefact from the cliff palace which we require back, you could never understand the power of that site and it's relics" Alex doesn't look worried at all which seems to make Achak uncomfortable "I have no idea what you are talking but don't worry I'll be out of the way soon" Awanyu steps forward right in front of Alex "Do not take us for fools we know you spent a night at the site alone and we know what you saw, you have no idea what you are dealing with and the damage your parents caused by removing the artefact" Alex who has had enough of the pair of them turns around and sits looking out of the window again "Why don't you both just fuck off I have no idea what you're talking about" At that the pair either decide to walk away and come up with another plan or just decide they are getting nowhere tonight, right now Alex doesn't really care, he's somewhere in between irritated and amused by the whole thing, but he's not being forced to leave by them.

Finishing his free drink courtesy of the snake god Awanyu he gets up and heads to the bar for another, just as he orders a beer, he spots them both huddled over a small table in the far corner of the bar and picks up the cocktail menu and orders two cocktails called Jesus Juice for them asking the barman to take them over for them. Claiming his window seat back and sitting looking at Achak and his friend as the barman takes two cocktails over, he raises his glass and takes a drink as the barman seems to have told them what the drinks were called. Being pretty sure it worked Alex sits laughing as the two of them stand up put their jackets on and leave very quickly, looking insane with anger but unable to do anything about it, Alex raises his glass to the barman with a grin that tells the barman it had the desired effect. Quietly sipping his beer safe in the knowledge that he'll be away from here and his unwanted friends soon. Finishing his beer and looking at the time, he leaves the bar and takes a slow walk back to the hotel, almost straining his neck to look at the stars, there isn't that many street lights around here so he can actually see all the stars clearly, probably the one thing he will miss about this place, but he has bigger fish to fry and a lot of work ahead of him if he wants answers to the mountain of questions he has. Deciding against a return trip to Cliff Palace, knowing they'll expect it, so best not kick the hornet's nest any more than he has. Over the next day he takes to the time to have a walk around the area and catch a few sights, not that there's much around apart the Mesa Verde.

CHAPTER 9

Waking up and checking the time, just after six, he's got some time before he needs to leave for his 10am flight, so he gets dressed and walks round to the breakfast room to at least have a coffee and a little breakfast, stopping at the reception on the way to get them to book him a cab to the airport. Walking into the breakfast room, which seems oddly quiet for the time of morning he grabs a coffee and some cereal and sits by the window. Not really paying much attention he doesn't notice much, just the winter sun which as usual is blinding and a few people walking around getting on with their daily business. Then the one thing he should have expected, his two shadows, which instantly makes him smile, wondering if they liked the Jesus Juice from the night before. Although he knows it's probably not wise to antagonize them, he just can't help himself, it's most fun he's had since trolling politicians on twitter got boring. Finishing his breakfast, he heads back round to his room to collect his bags before his cab arrives, waving at the black Mercedes parked in the car park on the way past.

Bags ready and checked out he stands in the fresh air waiting for his cab, it doesn't take long before it pulls in, ready to take him back to the airport to get out of here and away from the two idiots sat in the black Mercedes.

Quietly sitting watching out of the window, still in love with the views around here, the journey doesn't seem to take long, but it always seems quicker getting home than it does getting to where ever you have gone. Thanking the driver and heading through check in and security which is nice and quick since there's no queues at the moment, what a shame it can't be like this all the time. Feeling a sense of relief as he sits down in the boarding lounge not realising just how much Achak and Awanyu had bothered him, but now he can get away from here and start working what to do next. Sat cursing his parents, who despite having very little to do with him through most of his adult life, knew enough to give him this one job to do, find out about the rock, they knew he wouldn't be able to rest until he had found out exactly what it is, whether that's through some childhood need to get their approval or something else it doesn't really matter, all he knows is he's in too deep now. After what seems like about four hours sat waiting the call finally goes out for business class to board, getting up and double checking he has everything he starts to walk over to the gate, then he sees it, Awanyu sitting waiting for the rest of the plane to board, it looks like he has a travel companion, at least he didn't book business class as well. Obviously, this rock has more meaning to them than maybe he gave it credit for and after the display he saw on his night time trip to cliff palace, his mind starts to wonder to what it could be. Walking onto the plane and finding his seat, he automatically pulls out his notepad to start looking through his notes, so far, he has a few ideas, but all of them seem so farfetched that he has issues with his scientific mind being able to rationalise what he's seen and what he thinks.

Putting the scientist on sabbatical for a bit as the plane starts its taxi down the runway, he starts thinking of some of the more outrageous ideas, a portal? But where to? Somewhere else on Earth? Or somewhere else completely? Looking through his notes everything seems to be leading to the portal idea, but what was the light that dropped into the well? A power source? Or was that the portal? And the lightning was the power source? Hard to say which of those is valid but he can't help but think more of a power source than the portal, the well itself seems more likely to be a portal, maybe some residual effects of the rock being down there for centuries. Now his mind starts to think back to finding a strong enough power source somewhere in the UK when he gets back, being back in contact with John could be a blessing, he has something on John that could be useful in acquiring what he needs. Back when they worked together at the Sizewell B nuclear plant John almost sent the whole thing full Chernobyl, luckily it was Alex that stepped in just before it was too late to reverse it and covered it up neatly for John, no one else knows and no one else needs to, that is if John agrees to the plan that Alex is starting to formulate in his head, which is where it will stay, putting this down on paper might not be a wise idea. Now all the needs to work out is how to get John to agree to some alone time in the Sizewell B test room, no questions asked.

With the plane in the air he pulls out his phone and goes back to the photo he took the night he was at cliff palace, zooming in on the image he has a better view of the plant life just outside the cave, none of it looks like anything he's seen either on documentaries or with his own eyes, the plants do not look like anything on Earth, which leads him back to all of the questions already in his head, but there won't be many answers yet, not until he can work out what happens if he powers the rock, in his more childish mind, the side of him that still wishes he could have been an astronaut, he still keeps thinking about a portal to another plant, but every time he starts thinking about that his scientific mind creeps back in and destroys the thought. The time will come when he will be able to answer the questions, he just has a little more work to do first. Just as he's starting to come back to Earth, Awanyu comes walking down the aisle of the plane, heading straight to Alex, who luckily notices and locks his phone before he reaches him and presses the button for service and orders a drink, at the same time reporting a passenger that is harassing him, which sets the stewardess in a straight bee line for Awanyu who is quickly sent back to his seat with a warning that if he appears in business class again he will be reported and arrested on landing in London. That should keep him out of the way for a bit at least.

Settling back down with his drink Alex goes back to the photo on his phone, which leaves him more or less convinced that he's staring at the image from another planet, looking at the cave wall there is a feature that he knows isn't from this planet, the walls of the cave are streaked with a blue material, much like we would expect to see with a quartz vein, but electric blue. Pulling out his notepad again he starts to make notes and despite his attempts to think about this scientifically which doesn't make any sense, all of the theories that could explain it are null and void, an Einstein-Rosen bridge would have to be in space, a matter transporter has been theorised and dumped so many times it almost feels like a B list celeb and the list goes on, all wonderfully imagined theories but all just that theories. Changing his mindset to the sort of thing he would look at when he was still at school on the other hand leaves him believing that not only is it another planet but that piece of rock sat in what is now his apartment does create some sort of portal, the how and why of that he will hopefully explain later, but for now he starts writing a shopping list of items he'll need when he gets access to the power he needs, a solid when not an if, one thing Alex has always been good at is getting what he wants by any means necessary, thankfully he's never had to hide a body or clean a crime scene up. First on his shopping are a camera drone, followed by two pairs of decent sunglasses, knowing full well that John will not leave him in a test room alone, one thing they have in common is a distinct lack of trust in each other, mainly John not trusting Alex, but that's not much of a surprise to Alex and right now his more ruthless mind is starting to kick in.

Not realising how long he'd been pouring over the photo on his phone and making notes, the food trolley starts rolling along the aisle, just at the same time as Awanyu, if that even is his name opens the curtain and tries to carefully make his way to Alex again. Alex hadn't noticed him this time but the stewardess did and quickly, making her way straight to him and sending him back through the curtain again but this time she will report it, which for Alex is good, it means he will have time when the plane lands to get out of the way while he's being questioned by police, but on the down side it does mean the police will probably want to talk to Alex shortly after, but he can deal with that later.

Finally having some food in front of him, he puts his notepad and his phone away and starts eating, thankfully business class food is a little more like food and not the slop that Awanyu will be tucking into, at that thought one of the mischievous smiles appears on his face, while he quietly thinks of how much he can make his stalkers life hell on UK soil. First things first will be getting back to the apartment and hiding the rock, the rest can be left in view, if there is anything that shouldn't be there, he has plausible deniability and can allow them to go, his only interest is in the rock, if he is right, he's not even sure how long he'll be around. Sitting back after his dinner and ordering another beer, he just passes the time by watching films and listening to music, pretty sure that his stalker friend won't come looking for him again during the flight and it doesn't seem to take long, well two and half films long, before the seat belt light pings on and the captain announces that they will shortly be landing at London Gatwick Airport, meaning that Alex can quickly disappear and get back to the apartment and away from Awanyu.

Landing in London the police board straight away and take Awanyu off the plane in cuffs, which fills Alex with happiness, then business class are allowed off the plane into a quiet Gatwick Airport. It's quick enough to get his bags and get through security and straight into a cab back to his apartment, before he can be stopped by anyone wanting to ask questions, that part he can do perfectly well in the apartment if necessary. For now, he can just sit and watch the familiar sites of London passing by for the next half an hour till he's home. By the time he finally arrives back at the apartment it's getting late and rather than thinking of any major plans about dealing with his next problem, John being the problem, he just wants to sit and have a drink and head to bed, wanting to be up early to hide the rock and clean the rest of the mess up from the broken cabinet, just in case the police come knocking on the door. Finishing his drink and heading straight through to the bedroom, getting undressed on the way and collapsing on to the bed, he tries to get to sleep but every time he closes his eyes, he sees the cave with the blue streaks along the walls, eventually after about an hour of tossing and turning he falls asleep.

CHAPTER 10

Waking the next morning a little more refreshed and less concerned about Awanyu after seeing an article in the news about a native American male wanted in the US for multiple crimes who has been sent straight back to the states, meaning he will be left alone at least for the time being. Although the fact that he followed him back to the UK has left him feeling more than a little confused and worried. Going straight to the kitchen and making a coffee, his mind is running full steam, putting his coffee on the table and switching the news on, he gets his laptop, phone and notepad, ready to start the next part of his plan. Looking through his notepad the first thing he wants to do is order the equipment he needs, remembering another item he'll need, which will probably be the costliest, an XRF analyser to attempt a test on the rock itself, since the last thing he wants to do is hand it to anyone else to have it tested. Then he remembers, he needs to hide the rock somewhere just in case the police turn up, although it is already in a bag in the cupboard so it should be fine, at least for now and he doesn't plan to be around long. Finding an XRF for just over £34,000 that won't take long to reach him, he starts looking for the drone, it doesn't take long to find it and place his order, since he doesn't really need to worry about money, he can actually get the better ones and he's always wanted a drone anyway it could be fun to fly around the office at NASA to see how many people are playing solitaire on those expensive computers, now is the next issue, access to a power source.

Sitting drinking his coffee looking out over the Thames, he starts working out what he is going to say to John and how to phrase it, sending him a text to see if he wants to come over for a drink, deciding it would be better discussed behind closed doors, rather than in public. Pulling out his laptop and sending the photo over from his phone, he opens the image up on his laptop so that he can have a better look, he would have done this before, but being in public most of the time and having people following him he didn't want to risk having the image on a bigger screen than his phone. Hunching over the laptop trying to look at the smaller details to try and work out where exactly the cave is, nothing looks like anything he's ever seen before, but he also hasn't been to Peru, so he does a quick reverse image search and the only thing that come up are images from an episode of Star Trek, the rock in the cave looks normal, like any other cave, but the blue streaks, almost like lightning bolts running along the cave walls in horizontal streaks, that is something he knows doesn't exist anywhere he's seen. Closing the laptop and picking up his phone, he has a reply from John, just saying "Send me the address and I'll be over at about five have some beers ready"

Deciding he should probably go and get some more drink and some snacks, walking through to the bedroom to get dressed his eyes drift to closed cupboard where the rock has been hidden, not sure whether he wants to look at it or not, deciding to leave it where it is for now, at least until his XRF turns up anyway and he's not sure whether he should show John yet or not, maybe better to see how the conversation goes first. As he heads out into the fresh air, the fresh cold air after being in Colorado, he can't help but look over his shoulder after being followed for the last 3 or 4 days. Shrugging his concerns away for now he takes the short walk round to the nearest supermarket, it doesn't take him long once he's inside, it never does, snacks and beers in his basket, he heads to the whiskey section and chooses a nice bottle of Highland Park. Paying as quickly as he can he walks straight back to the apartment, with about an hour before John appears he really should clean up what's left of the glass on the floor. Putting the food and beers away and cleaning the glass up, he sits at the table by the window with his notepad out and a can in his hand, staring out at the Thames writing down tests he wants to carry out before he gets to the power plant, if he can force John's hand. A car battery test would be a good start, that might work well depending on if his theories are right and that it really does open a portal of some sort. Not realising the time, the buzzer for the downstairs door goes and almost makes him spit beer all over the table, walking over to the camera to make sure it is John, he presses the button to let him in, for the first time he starts feeling nervous, he has to get this right to get access, otherwise he has a lot more to work out and a person that knows too much, that will need convincing to stay quiet.

Just as John reaches out to knock on the door, Alex swings it open and shows him in, grabbing two cold beers from the fridge on the way over to the sofa, as they both sit down John goes straight in with a question Alex should have expected, what is this about? Trust being the issue again, Alex turns to face him taking a large drink of beer "OK I had hoped to break this a little easier but since you ask, I need access to the test room at Sizewell B" John actually for once looks shocked at something Alex has said, normally he would just accept it as being Alex. "What the fuck do you want that for? You haven't even bothered to ask how things have been going there" Alex laughs, something that John is used to, a rare laugh that Alex has when he feels uncomfortable "There is something my parents left for me, among many other things in this apartment but I need to run some tests on one of them and I need power to do it, I can show you but if you say a word I will end you and you know I can" John just sits for a minute, seemingly thinking about his next answer "OK show me and then we'll talk about it" At that Alex gets up and makes his way to the bedroom, trying to think of his next step, although he doesn't have much of a choice, he may as well tell John what he knows, it might be the only way he can get him on board.

Carrying the rock through in its foil cocoon, he carefully places it on the floor where the cabinet used to sit, "I can't put it anywhere else if I'm to show you it can't be near a power source so I'd leave your phone over there and if you still wear it your hearing aid too" John places his phone on the table and pulls a small hearing aid from his left ear and places that down too, looking more than a little confused and walks over to where Alex is standing. Without saying a word Alex bends down and carefully removes the foil to reveal the black rock. John bends slowly to look closer, stretching his hands out to touch it he looks up at Alex "What is it? It feels I don't know alive? Electric?" Alex signals for him to come and sit at the sofa again, suddenly his mouth is dry and he needs a drink to continue, they both sit as Alex goes on to tell John pretty much everything he has found out so far, finishing by pulling his laptop over and opening the image of the cave up to show him "Where is this? It doesn't look like anywhere I recognise" Alex taking another a big drink tries to explain the best he "I don't think this is anywhere, anyone has seen, I don't think it's Earth and that's why I need secrecy and power" John turns to look back at the rock "I don't think I can help" Alex doesn't give him chance to say anymore "I thought you might say that at first but remember when we were both working at Sizewell and you almost sent it full Chernobyl until I jumped in and saved your ass and buried the truth? I'd hate for that to come out in the open it could be very bad for your career" John's shoulders slumps and he takes a drink "I would have said you wouldn't but I know you well enough to know that you would without hesitation, I need to make a call tomorrow and I'll let you know and yes before you say it I will keep my mouth shut is there anything else or should I leave now" Alex smiles a little "Don't feel you have to leave you can stay for a drink if you like I'd love to hear your ideas on this" John obviously doesn't want much more to do with it right now and gets up grabbing his jacket on the way to the door "I'll message you tomorrow" At that he walks out which doesn't really bother Alex, who after a tense couple of hours winning John around, if that's what you can call it anyway, could do with a much stronger drink and goes to pour himself a neat whiskey, it won't do any good watering it down with anything, not even ice.

Sitting back at the table by the window looking out at the Thames again, he suddenly starts to miss Cortez, there he could sit and watch the stars, here on the other hand he can't see a single star through all the light pollution, then his mind starts to wonder what the stars and planets would look like from another planet? Is it even the solar system? It would be incredible to be able to watch the stars and planets of somewhere else. Suddenly remembering the rock is still sat in the middle of the floor he goes to wrap it back up and hide it again, since there is still a high chance that the police could come knocking, but he thinks that would have already happened if it was going to and with his stalker back in the US and probably in a cell it's doubtful the police will bother.

With the rock out of sight again and it being dark outside he decides to take the bottle of whiskey and some cans and go and lay in bed and watch some films, despite not replacing his parent's bed he doesn't really mind now, something in his train of thought to do with his parents seems to have changed without him noticing. Laying on the bed watching Marvel's Endgame for what must been the 15th time if not more, he slowly sips at his whiskey and has an odd thought that makes him laugh, if it really is another planet, he'll need plenty of whiskey to take with him till he can learn to brew it himself, maybe he should research that too. With the travel and everything else recently it doesn't take him long to drift off to sleep and he doesn't wake up until his phone pings just after 10am the next morning.

Sitting up on the edge of the bed rubbing his eyes he and reads the message from John "12pm Saturday I've got us an hour in the test room" 3 days and he can see what real power does to the rock. His equipment should be delivered today, which gives him time to set it up and test it before his road trip with John. For the rest of the day, it will probably be eating, drinking and watching films, since he can't really go out until his deliveries have arrived and right now, he has no interest in going out, unless that is he needs more food or drink, forgetting about the car battery idea he doesn't need that now. Looking for something to watch, not really being rushed for time he decides to start the Marvel films again from the beginning, of course skipping Hulk, he never liked that film, it's doubtful even marvel liked that one.

Around 4pm the door buzzer goes and looking at the camera, it's his delivery and suddenly he feels like a little kid again and almost punches the button to open the door and then stands there with the apartment door open waiting. As soon at the driver gets upstairs, he takes all the parcels, signs for them and promptly closes the door. Taking the parcel with the XRF in it, he wants to set that one up first, he needs to know what the rock is made of and his geeky side has always wanted to use one of these. Sitting on the sofa he opens the box up and grabs the manual and reads the sections he needs to, setting it up he goes to get a fork to test it with, placing the fork on the table he picks up the XRF and holds it to the fork and the readings come out exactly as he'd expect, now the bigger item needs to be checked, fetching the rock from the cupboard again he places it on the floor, planning to be able to leave it in the foil, the XRF should see through it, he just needs to ignore the aluminium, although he knows that isn't really shielding it very well, he could really do with a lead lined box, every time he passes with anything that has power he feels the atmosphere change a little.

Picking up the XRF his hands start to shake, steadying himself he holds the XRF slightly away from the foil and holds the trigger down, waiting for the readings which seem to take forever, then the bleep to say it's done and he sits back looking at the readings with a look of complete confusion. Platinum, Gold, Mercury, Iron, Silicon, Titanium and a very high concentration of something unknown, 58% of something unknown makes no sense and the next thing that comes to mind is those blue streaks in the cave walls, could it be that? A completely new element.

CHAPTER 11

Still confused about the XRF readings, he starts to look at the drone, hoping he'll be able to get some more of an idea of where that cave is at the test on Saturday, if he can truly open a portal of some sort. Putting the drone on charge he sits at the table and opens up his laptop again to attempt to try to find what the mix of metals could be, whether it could be a manufactured alloy or something completely different, unable to find anything that could even be a close match, he starts to think of other problems he could have. Can he use the drone through a portal? Will the batteries die? Or will he just lose signal? Then probably the biggest question he has in his head, can he step through the portal? The look of the plant life and general clear air looks OK but the only way he can really know is either to step through himself or send someone else and he doesn't think that John would agree to that and he certainly isn't telling anyone else, he already has too many people in the loop and that's just John, Awanyu and Achak.

Looking over at the drone with its green light flashing to tell him it's ready and picks it up, stepping out on to the balcony, the weathers calm, so it's time for a test flight, setting it down on the table and studying the controls for a minute, he slowly starts to float it just above the table and move it around a little, seems easy enough. Next over the balcony railing, looking at the screen on his controller the camera is crystal clear, next step drop down a little maybe look through downstairs window, which he quickly realises was a mistake, looking at the camera, he sees an overweight grey haired man slumped on the sofa with just a laptop to cover his modesty, quickly bringing the drone back up and on to his side of the railing, with an image that will be burnt into his memory forever, he considers that test flight to be plenty, not wanting to risk seeing any more than he already has, taking the drone back inside and taking a mouthful of beer, it could take years to get that vision out of his head if he ever can.

Having tested out the new equipment his attention turns back to the rock, trying to think of ways to test its properties and try to attempt to identify it, which may prove difficult, all he knows at the moment is that it could be something to do with the blue streaks on the cave wall. The first thing he can think of is to see if it reacts to a magnet, pulling out his phone and slipping it out of its case so he can use the magnet on his phone case to see what happens, slowing moving the magnet to the rock, it instantly sticks to the side of the rock with more force than he would have expected from such a small magnet. Writing down his findings he sits on the sofa trying to work out what to do next, he has got 3 days and has very little he can do until he gets a better power source.

Deciding he would be better trying to go through his notes and do some more research on the Anasazi, he settles on the sofa with his laptop and notepad and starts searching for more information, it seems almost impossible to date the rock or come up with any new ideas on it. The Anasazi are known to be around from 1000 BCE till present day in one way or another, which doesn't narrow anything down, also the fact that they appear to have no direct trade links with any other culture. The Anasazi themselves as history knows them all but vanished around 1130 CE, which leaves Alex with a huge amount of time to look at, which seems almost pointless, the chance of finding anything relevant to the rock seems like a one in a million shot. Deciding that the amount of work he would need to put in for little reward is a waste of time, which leaves him a couple of days to fill and now that he's not being stalked by Native Americans, he feels a little safer leaving the building, first stop is somewhere nice for dinner, after that maybe a few drinks and a little site seeing, that should at least fill 2 days, putting the idea of the car battery test to rest, not wanting to risk too much in the apartment.

CHAPTER 12

After wasting the last couple of days wandering around London taking in a few sites and more than a few pints it's finally Friday evening, this feels like the most important day for a long time, but he has no idea why, just one of those gut feelings that tells him this is crucial to everything else. Pouring a whisky, he sits back on the sofa and puts the news on, it's been a few days since he's bothered checking what's happening in the world, mainly Covid still and rumours that Russia are up to something, which is no surprise to him. He doesn't really take much of the news in, his head is still racing with thoughts of Saturday, John will be picking him about 9am to head to the Sizewell plant and the test on the rock, any number of things could go wrong, but as far as Alex is concerned it's worth the risk. Sitting back lost in thoughts sipping at his drink trying to get his thoughts in order and try to stop himself thinking about some of the more theoretical ideas time passes quickly and he decides just to go and get some sleep, ready for tomorrow, heading to bed he takes a quick look in the cupboard, one last look at the rock in its foil, but before he goes to sleep he remembers he needs a lead lined container, finding a lead lined camera bag from a site that can do a delivery within the M25 by 9am, he orders it straight away and rolls over to get some sleep.

Waking up at 7am Saturday morning and putting the kettle on for his morning coffee, he switches the news on, nothing much that hasn't been going around the last year or two, but it's only really on for background noise. Making his coffee and sitting at the table in front of the windows looking out over the Thames he starts to think about what all of this could mean, what if it really is a portal? Does he stay or does he risk going through? He has no family contact and very few people he could call friends, so why not? Finishing his coffee and getting dressed, he starts getting other bits ready, the rock and the drone, just as he puts his bags by the door the buzzer for the door goes, a quick glance at the camera and he sees a delivery driver, letting him in he stands with the door open and almost snatches the box and quickly moves the rock into its new home. Before he can relax, he takes his phone and holds it against the bag and breathes a sigh of relief when nothing happens. As he's just about to put his phone away his phone pings, John is outside and ready to go. Picking up his bags and heading downstairs in the lift it suddenly dawns on him, this could be life changing, so far the whole experience since finding the note from his parents has been lifechanging, but this could be huge. Walking out of the lift and putting his bags in the boot of John's car and climbing in the passenger seat, the first thing he notices is the colour of John's skin, he looks pale, like he's about to faint "Are you ok?" John just nods and starts driving, Alex judging the mood in the car doesn't say a word, waiting for John to say something or ask a question, you could cut the air with a knife. Then suddenly John blurts it out "You know I could lose my job for this?" Alex had thought about that, but Alex being Alex, he has something he needs to do and anything that happens is collateral damage "I had thought about that but don't forget if you hadn't done this, you'd probably lose your job anyway this is something huge that we can't just ignore if this is what I think you can come with me" John looks to his left, a little colour starting to come across his face "Come with you? What are you talking about?" Alex just laughs "You'll see" At that John puts the music on and the two just continue the drive, neither man was much for small talk anyway so this sort of silence between them is perfectly normal.

A couple of hours later they arrive at the main gate for the power plant, pulling out his I.D. card the security guard opens the gate and lets them through watching Alex as they go, trying to work out why John is bringing a guest to a nuclear power station on a Saturday. Parking up Alex goes to the boot pulling out the case with the drone and the other bag, which has the rock and a notebook in, John just ignores him and keeps walking. Entering through the main doors and heading straight down a corridor, following the signs for research and test rooms, walking down the corridor seems to take a lifetime, it's been a few years since Alex was here and he forget how much walking he used to do. After about 10 minutes of snaking corridors, they finally reach the test room, both men grab a white jacket and walk in. The minute they get in there Alex puts the bag down on the table and carefully lifts the rock out and places it down on the floor next to a set of test ports, then he grabs two cables that hang on the walls when not in use, this place hasn't changed one bit. Plugging the cables in to the test sockets it almost looks like he's getting ready to jump start a car. Placing the other end of the cables down one either side of the bag, he tells John to stand by the control panel, as he gets the drone out and ready. He suddenly starts to wonder; will he be able to send the drone through without it destroying the battery? That doesn't really matter right now, he's here now too late to worry about any of that. 5 minutes and the drone is ready to fly, making sure he's far enough away from the rock that he can avoid frying the batteries before he even gets started he places the drone down and walks back to the rock "Get ready John I'm taking it out" John's complexion has turned to a nice shade of grey, taking a large gulp he places his hand on the dial to set the power, as Alex makes his way back to the drone and picks the controller up, he looks down at the display and he's happy to at least see that the rock hasn't drained the batteries yet "John turn it to a quarter power for a start please" John carefully turns the dial a quarter of the way round and almost instantly they see a circular black orb floating a couple of inches off the floor, probably big enough to fly the drone through, but that's not what Alex is looking for "John up to half please" John not saying a word turns the dial to the half power mark and both of them stop dead in their tracks, the orb is now almost big enough to walk through crouching, but that's not what has them both staring in either shock or awe, in awe for Alex but with John it's much more likely to be shock and a little fear.

They are staring through a perfectly round portal, staring at the inside of a cave, Alex picks up the drone's controller "Here goes Johnny this is what we have been waiting for" floating the drone off the floor he slowly starts to move forward expecting to the see it just drop to the floor with drained batteries, but it doesn't the power going directly to the rock must be enough to keep it stable. Flying forward the drone floats right in front of the portal and with one last push forward it slips through, looking at the screen on the controller Alex can see the cave walls crystal clear and those blue streaks, which almost seem to the pulsing, flying the drone slowly through the cave with the video recording, he turns the camera left to right making sure he has a good video of everything, as the drone starts to close in on the mouth of the cave, Alex almost drops the control, this is the first time he is almost certain this is not on Earth, then from behind "What do you see?" Alex jumps a little, concentrating so hard he almost forgot John was still in the room "I'll show you once we're out of here, I can't risk anyone seeing this" Flying the drone back through and landing it in front of him John moves forward a little "Power down?" Alex shakes his head "Not yet one more thing" Alex takes a few steps forward, standing right in front of the portal, he can feel the hairs on the back of his hands and arms standing up, with a deep breath he leans forward, an arm goes through first "Well that was fine" as John steps forward "Be careful you don't know what you're doing" Pulling his arm back he takes one small step forward and leans toward the portal, slowly his head slips through. John can only stand a look with horror on his face, then slowly Alex's head comes back through "Are you fucking insane you could have killed yourself" Alex lets out a laugh "But I didn't turn it up full, I need to see what power I'll need" John compliant as always walks back and turns the power up, as soon as he does the portal suddenly spreads putting two of the test room windows out and setting off alarms everywhere. Without saying a word both men jump into action, Alex grabbing the drone and John switching the power off, grabbing the rock both men walk out of the room, trying their hardest to pretend nothing happened, everybody is too busy trying to work out what the alarm is for, that they barely notice the two men walking toward the exit at the back of the building wanting to get outside as quick as they can. 10 minutes later their back in John's car "Fuck if I lose my job I swear" cut off by Alex "You swear what? You can't do anything I have too much information, some of it could put you in jail and you know that" Starting the drive towards the exit, they get stopped at the gate and the security guard pulls John's ID card from his neck "We'll be in touch now go" as they drive out John falls stone cold silent, not talking all the way back, as they finally pull up back outside Alex's London apartment, Alex breaks the silence "Come upstairs and I'll show you the video, trust me it will be worth it" John turns to look and sees a look on Alex's face that he doesn't recognise, excitement, but almost manic excitement. Walking in to the building and up in the lift they head straight to the kitchen, Alex grabbing them both a can from the fridge and quickly turns his laptop on and removes the memory card from the drone, plugging it into the laptops card slot. John is looking over Alex's shoulder, deadly quiet, taking a large drink as Alex opens up the video and starts it playing. Both men stand in amazement as the drone's video moves closer to the cave entrance "What the fuck?" Alex smiles "I might have something more interesting for you to do instead of working at that power station any longer" John stands back shaking his head "I won't go with you I won't say a word to anyone but I won't go with you I have my family do what you want but leave me out of this" Alex looking shocked and disappointed "Wow John, I always knew you were a fucking fairy but seriously you want to pass this up? You don't even have a job now" At that John just puts his drink down grabs his jacket and walks out of the apartment, leaving Alex a little bewildered and really pissed off, but one little set back won't stop him. Now he has to come up with a plan, he knows he can breathe the air and he knows enough to know he can walk through the portal without harm.

CHAPTER 13

With John out of the equation Alex has found himself at a bit of a loose end, he has to follow this through, that's why his parents left him the note, because they knew he wouldn't be able to give up on it, not for any sentimental reason, just because they know what he's like. Sitting looking on the internet, trying to find out somewhere he could go for a strong enough power source, he remembers something from his work for the European Space Agency, a rumoured bunker in Siberia, luckily for Alex he never really left any job empty handed, he still has a stash of memory sticks only he knows about, some from NASA, some of the ESA, it might have been worth the risk now, because god knows the risk was big enough, stealing secrets, probably espionage or spying, the consequences could have ended him. Going through to the bedroom he picks up his bag from the corner and pulls out a small metal case and takes it back to the table. Opening it up there is close to 50 memory sticks all neatly ordered and numbered, thanks to a good memory he plucks out one marked 38 and sticks it into the laptop, quickly scanning through the files, he finds the one he needs, a file on someone called Petrov Nikitin, ex KGB, now part of Russia's nuclear planning committee. All he needed was the name, even Russia's top people have email addresses somewhere on the internet.

Sitting trying to think of alternatives, working with the Russians would have always been a serious last resort, but let's face it, the UK or more to the point any other country would instantly want complete access and he probably wouldn't even be involved, they'd take the artefact and send him packing. As long as he sells it right, he might, just might be able to get access and he's got a better idea of how to play ball with the Russians and if he's right, he won't be around much longer. Looking at the e-mail address in front of him, his only thought as he starts typing is, fuck it what else can I do?

Subject: Private Project

Mr Nikitin

My name is Alex Mackintosh, a while ago working for the ESA, I found some information with your name attached relating to a nuclear reactor based in a remote location in Siberia. I am interested in being able to use this place for a private project than may benefit both me and Russia, I have some information you may find useful as payment.

Alex

Pausing just before he clicks the send button "Fuck it" Closing the laptop he walks to the kitchen and pours a nice large whisky, needing something to take the edge off. Sitting staring out at the Thames, sipping at his whisky with no idea what to do next, all he can do is sit and wait for a reply, which he isn't expecting too soon if at all.

The chances of him receiving a reply are slim, as he sits looking at the Thames, gathering his thoughts and trying to work out a plan B, his phone pings, picking it up in a rush just to see a spam e-mail. Thinking about plan B everything is coming up blank, China, he trusts even less than the Russians and his main point is that the Russians have an isolated nuclear reactor in the middle of Siberia, some of the information he gained from his work is finally coming to use. The Russians believe no one knows about the bunker housing a nuclear reactor, at least as far as Alex knows it's just a reactor, but most of the western world know about the bunker. As for plan B, he doesn't have one so here's hoping the information he is willing to share with the Russians as payment will be enough, if not he has a major issue, for a start the Russians will know a British man wants access to a nuclear reactor and the second issue is that they will know he has information and whatever happens they will want it.

Sitting staring out at the Thames, wondering what to do, his mind has been running at full speed since all of this started and now all he can do is wait, something he's never been good at. He can't open the portal without a power and he can't get access to power without help, the only thing left to do is grab the bottle of whisky and a glass and sit and at least attempt to relax a bit on the sofa or just drink the bottle and pass out so he doesn't need to think of the implications of the decision he has made. Putting a film on and pouring a large whisky he still can't quieten his mind and starts looking at the image of the inside of the cave, zooming in and out on each part of the image, the blue streaks in the rock, the plants at the cave entrance, the more he looks the more convinced he is that where ever the cave is, it is almost certainly not on Earth, then he notices something else, something that amazes him and leaves his terrified in equal measure, a single painted symbol, just at the cave entrance. He didn't get a clear enough image to see what it is, but he knows it's not natural, someone or something has put it there. just what the fuck were his parents doing with the rock? Putting his phone down on the table, trying to concentrate on the film, a sudden wave of tiredness hits him and he decides on a nap on the sofa to try and waste away some of the day. The next thing he knows is being woken up by the door buzzer at 10am, jumping up and looking at the camera, he sees someone carrying a package of some sort, but he hasn't ordered anything else, buzzing him in he waits for him to come to the door, the first thing he notices when he opens the door is a Russian accent as he gets a piece of paper pushed at him "Sign here" signing for the package and handing the paper back, he closes the door and goes back to the sofa, staring at the box, it has no name or address on it, nothing just a blank box. Opening it up carefully his look of confusion deepens as he pulls out a phone, nothing fancy just a plain mobile phone, the most it would have on it is snake, under the phone is a note "Turn on and wait" at that his heart starts beating a little faster and little harder, it has to be from the Russians, now the nerves start, was that e-mail really the way to deal with this? He suddenly gets a sense of dread, but then his more ruthless side starts to kick back in, so what, what did he expect? An e-mail reply about a secret nuclear reactor in Siberia? The Russians will do everything to cover their tracks, but that's the part that makes him nervous.

CHAPTER 14

Turning the phone on and going to make a coffee, he sits back on the sofa with the phone on the table in front of him, not even sure how long he's supposed to wait, probably until the delivery driver has notified them that he has delivered the package. Just as he sits back trying to avoid staring at the phone, just as he turns the TV on, the phone rings, a withheld number, no surprise there. Answering with just a hello, a thick Russian accent comes through "Hello Mr Mackintosh my name is Petrov" Alex's nerves hit the roof "Er yeah hi" Petrov's voice comes through as quite harsh and to the point "Let's discuss your needs, you will understand the secrecy of me sending a burner phone for this but what exactly prompted you to ask about a power source for a private matter?" Alex takes a deep breath and steadies himself, ready to be either blown out of the water or worse "Yes I have a private matter, a project that I require some power for, I am aware of a nuclear reactor somewhere in a Siberian bunker and I have some information that I think you would be interested in as payment" The line goes quiet, almost to a point of Alex thinking that Petrov has hung up, then he comes back to life and speaks quieter than before "I see, you obviously know enough about the bunker in Siberia to know it will suit your needs and looking through your information from my research on you I can guess how you found out about it. Now the question is what exactly do you have as payment that you would risk working with us over your own government?" Now that he has his attention Alex starts to settle more into the conversation "Well I have around about 50 memory sticks of information taken from various agencies that should interest you I'm willing to part with them on agreement from yourself that I have private unmonitored use of the bunker and anything that my research throws up that may be of use to you I will share if I go through my own government they will want too much control" Again that deafening silence comes through, but this is sensitive, so I guess he should have expected it "I am intrigued now Mr Mackintosh you are willing to trust Russians over your own and willing to sell secrets for your needs tell me something you have that would be of interest and we will see what we can arrange" Alex sits in silence this time trying to think of something worthwhile "Well there is a matter of the international space station and America planning to decommission it with your astronauts still on board" No silence this time "OK here's how this is going to work you have your access but you will need to leave tomorrow and tell no one I will arrange a car to take you to a private airstrip and you will travel to the Russian embassy in Moscow for a meeting and exchange of information with me directly and assuming your payment is enough you will be flown to the bunker no questions asked" Alex with no other option now agrees to the terms and Petrov hangs up immediately.

Putting the phone back down on the table, his hands are shaking and his heads trying to beat the 4-minute mile record, pouring a whisky needing something to settle his nerves, he takes a sip and sits with his hands on his head trying to work out what he needs to do. As he calms down, he starts planning what to take, at least there shouldn't be much airport security to avoid, getting up and finding a suitcase in his parent's cupboard he starts packing his clothes putting the foil wrapped rock in the middle for padding, then the back of memory sticks stashed in a jumper, looking around there doesn't seem to be much else that he will need apart from his phone, laptop and his senses. Just as he zips up his case there's a ping from the burner phone "Be ready at 7am" short and sweet but he didn't even expect to get that much from Petrov. He knows the risks of playing with the Russians but he's always been hard headed and goal driven and his only goal is to find out for definite what the portal is and where it leads, his one remaining problem is that he still doesn't know what to do after that. Whatever happens now is out of his hands, he's already committed to working with the Russians and there's nothing he can do to change that, they will want the information and whether that's by Alex's means or the Russians, they will get it one way or another and he'd rather be alive to finish his project so leaving his case at the door and settling back on the sofa with the burner phone on the table just in case it goes off again and pours another whisky before he finds a film to watch and just waste the hours till he goes bed. Two films later and the tiredness starts again, not wanting to sleep on the sofa for a second night he pours one last whisky and heads through to the bedroom. The minute his head hits the pillow his mind kicks in again, a million questions with no answers. Is this the best choice he could have made? What happens when he gets through the portal? And of course, the one thing that's been in the back of his mind ever since finding the note from his parents and started looking into the origins and purpose of the rock, are his parents alive?

CHAPTER 15

Waking up at 5am after finally drifting off to sleep, the first he needs is coffee, so he sluggishly makes his way to the open plan kitchen taking a glance at his suitcase by the front door, coffee in hand he sits on the sofa, trying hard to wake up properly before the car turns up. For some reason the nerves have vanished and things actually start to feel right, like this is the right decision and even if it isn't he's stuck with it now. Finishing his coffee and picking up a backpack he slides his laptop and chargers inside and sits back on the sofa again, checking the time, 6.45am, 15 minutes to go then all control will sit with the Russians which is probably the worst part of it for Alex, he's always been in control of what happens, so the thought of relinquishing any control is scary let alone all control, but between now and getting to the bunker, if he makes it that far, all control is in the Russians hands.

Having a quick look around the apartment, he can't see anything that he's forgotten, just then the buzzer goes and he almost jumps off the sofa, walking to the door and looking at the camera, it's the same person that delivered the burner phone, which is in the opposite pocket to his own phone. Picking up his case and backpack he leaves the apartment and makes his way downstairs to the waiting car outside, walking out into a freezing morning in London, if he wasn't awake before he sure as hell is now, the driver opens the back door of a black Mercedes just as one thought enters his mind and he has to stifle a laugh, why is it always a black Mercedes? Sitting in back of the car with a dividing screen between him and the driver, who so far hasn't said a word, he starts to question himself again, is this really the best idea he could have come up with? His impulses drive him and sometimes taking a step back and thinking before he acts would probably help a lot at times. Driving through London all he can do is look out of the window and catch some of the sights on the way, it doesn't take long to get out of London and start driving down the motorway, half an hour later and they're driving through the unmanned gates of a private airstrip, one that he's pretty sure he's never heard of or seen on a map. The car pulls up alongside a private jet, which reminds him of all those Hollywood films where the main protagonist always seems to have a sparkling clean private jet, being ushered onto the plane by the silent Russian driver he walks up the steps and walks into an open lounge with seats that would probably cost as much as his flat in Edinburgh and a bottle of whisky and two glasses on the table, the driver hasn't boarded and he's the only person on the plane that he can see, so why two glasses?

Just as he sits down pondering whether to pour a drink or wait to see if anyone joins him, the door to the plane starts to close and the engines start up just as the cockpit door opens and a middle age man steps through, a scar running down one side of his face, makes him look more menacing than the rest of his body seems to, about five and a half feet tall, a slim muscular figure that obviously takes more time than Alex would bother with to maintain. Without saying a word, he slides into the opposite seat and pours two whiskies, which makes Alex feel a little better, in his head Alex is sitting there thinking well he wouldn't kill me and waste the whisky. They both take a drink, for Alex that's to settle the uneasy feeling of no one saying a word since he left the flat, which reminds him of several ex's before breakups, that killer silent treatment where you're not sure if they are planning a slow and gruesome death or something much worse, then finally he talks, in a thick Russian accent that Alex recognises instantly, which makes his anxiety go full blast, why is Petrov Nikitin sat facing me when we were going to meet at the Russian embassy?

"May I call you Alex and break the formalities?"

Alex nods "Is the same OK for you?"

"Of course now I know we we're going to meet at the embassy but we can talk a little more privately here, as well as no one trusting the Russians, not even the Russians trust the Russians if you understand my meaning?"

"Completely"

"So, let's get to business, shall we? It doesn't take long to fly to Moscow and we have much to discuss. Why exactly do you need access to a Russian bunker in the middle of Siberia when your own country has several nuclear reactors at their disposal?"

"Well it's all a matter of trust and privacy I have been working on a private project that I require a power source for and I would rather not disclose all the details until I have had the time to work on it but it could be very beneficial to both parties, myself and who ever allows me the access I require"

Petrov pauses for a minute thinking over what he has just been told "Well in that case depending on the information you have for us I'm sure we could make arrangements"

At that Alex lays his suitcase on the floor of the plane and pulls out a bag, tipping the memory sticks out onto the table "There's around 50 here years of information that I'm sure you could make use of"

"Secrets for access a very Russian move" Pulling

a panel in the bottom of his seat Petrov pulls a laptop up and sets it down so they can both see, Alex pushes one memory stick toward him that he quickly plugs into the laptop, pulling up the first file he pauses to read "Ah the ISS information so the UK, USA and everyone else involved with the space station are planning to launch a nuclear missile to destroy the station with our astronauts on board and then blame Russia as a way of stopping our involvement and this is to happen in 2025? How do I know this is genuine?"

"You read correctly and if you analyse the file you will see the proof of its origin and there are plenty more like that for you to see"

Another long pause before Petrov starts talking again "OK I will take your word that these are genuine and I have no interest as to how you got so much information out, I will allow your access but you must understand that this means you can have no further contact with anyone apart from us for security reasons you understand?"

"I have no one I would share this with and when the time is right I will discuss what I have been working on with you, but that is my terms just believe me when I say this will be very beneficial to Russia"

"OK we understand each other when we land you will be taken to the embassy for a few hours and then you will be flown to the bunker later this evening it makes it easier if we can have deniability of you being involved with us" at that Alex holds his hand out as a sign of trust, Petrov quickly shakes his hand and looks out of the window "Ah mother Russia we are almost here I will leave you to finish your whisky" Petrov stands after gathering all the memory sticks up in the bag and puts his laptop back under his seat and makes his way to the cockpit, leaving Alex to breathe a sigh of relief and take a large mouthful of whisky to steady his nerves, that was unexpected but very fruitful, he has a feeling that the worst is out of the way.

10 minutes later the plane starts to descend as Alex looks out of the window as Moscow comes into view, it looks nicer than he thought it would, but there won't be any sightseeing for Alex, just the embassy then off to Siberia and time to work on what exactly the rock is and more importantly where it leads. Sitting thinking about it he suddenly has this giddy sort of optimism about the future and has no idea why. Landing in Moscow the minute he steps out of the plane door he realises he really did not come kitted out for Russian weather, but he's instantly ushered into a car with blacked out windows, another black Mercedes, not much of a stereotype there, but at least this one has a small mini fridge and a bottle of whisky, maybe the Russians are following their own stereotypes and providing whisky for the

Scottish man. Sitting back in the car watching out of the windows the burner phone pings "I won't see you again before your flight to Siberia I have arranged some warmer clothes for you if you need equipment, you will have access to a secure private e-mail system at the bunker" short and sweet but he didn't expect much else. Picking up his other phone to check the news and the first thing he sees makes his heart sink a little, he already knows what has happened without any context, the headline reads **London man found dead suspected poisoning.** He hadn't thought of the prospect of the Russians making sure he had no loose ends, but there is little he can do now that will make any difference, for now he's just glad he didn't talk to anyone else.

CHAPTER 16

Half an hour later they pull up at the back of the embassy in a secure carpark and he is ushered straight through to a private room, the Russians certainly don't want him to be seen. Walking into the room his eyes light up at a table full of food and a fridge filled with drink, it feels like he hasn't eaten for about a week, which isn't far off considering he's been eating snacks and junk for the last week or so and drinking more than he usually would, but he can blame that on stress. Being left in the room alone he suddenly starts to feel a little vulnerable, before although he was dealing with the Russians, he had distance in his corner but now he's sat in the Russian embassy in Moscow with no one to turn to for help or advice and no way of backing out of what he started, for Alex this is new and feels very uncertain, no matter what he has done in the past he's already had control over the situation, but this, he has no control of anything.

Half an hour later he hears a knock at the door and Petrov comes walking through with a smile on his face, but there is something deeper in that smile, an understanding maybe? Or maybe just the realisation that he has enough information to destabilise Europe. Sitting down opposite Alex, Petrov starts straight away "I have to say Alex even I am shocked at the information you have given us enough information to completely derail most of Europe this must mean a lot to you, we agreed no information about your project would be discussed until you have results and I will respect that, what you have given us is more than payment enough for what you need" At that Petrov holds a hand out, which settles some of Alex's nerves, knowing that he has what he needs from the Russians with no questions asked. The two shake hands and Petrov pulls out a small envelope "In here is a sim card I need you to hand me yours from your phone from this moment on you disappear" That statement hits him harder than he expected, sliding his phone out of his pocket and taking the sim card out a lyric from a song springs to mind "This is where I disappear" and he hands his sim to Petrov who without a second look cuts it into two pieces and drops it in the bin and hands Alex the new sim "You understand why we have to do this?" a nod from Alex is all Petrov needs "You will be leaving here at 6am to make the journey to your new home I suggest you eat and get some rest before tomorrow" at that Petrov gets up and leaves him sat alone, locking the door on the way out, no windows and the only way out is locked, well at least he's secure. There's a bathroom to the side and a sofa bed, so this is it until the morning, just Alex trapped in a room with nothing more than his own thoughts to keep him company, at least he has his phone and the bag with his laptop in and a Wi-Fi password taped to the coffee table. Pulling out his laptop the first thing he does is open the image of the cave, zooming in as far as he can on the cave entrance, he sits staring at the look of the plants and trees that he can see, for some reason every time he opens the image up, he gets more and more confused and he starts to realise how Alice felt going down the rabbit hole, but seems like a fucking big rabbit hole. Then he starts to run back through the conversation with Petrov, he has disappeared but what does that mean? Will he even be allowed to go back to any normal life? Or going to his worse fear is his only way out to hope he can live wherever the portal leads? For now all he can do is wait and try to read between the lines to try and work out Petrov's motives.

Looking around the room, mainly at the fridge in the corner, setting his eyes on the bottle of vodka, instantly thinking, who puts vodka in the fridge? Getting up and taking the bottle and a glass he sits back on the sofa bed and pulls the coffee table in front of him to rest his laptop on, time for some games, something to pass the time and instantly opens up Minecraft, something relaxed but something to focus on away from the intrusive thoughts in his head. Sitting playing and drinking vodka helps clearing his head and then the realisation hits him, as a child all he wanted was to see the stars, his mum used to take him outside at night, usually bad nights full of nightmares and they would sit and look at the stars and she would always ask him what he thought those distance stars would look like, every star is another sun with another galaxy circling it, a billion possibilities. When he would answer his mum, it was always a child's imagination of strange looking animals and humanoid aliens like he'd see on TV and robots for some reason always robots. Now he may have a way to fulfil those dreams, he's worrying about what happens here but if he's right he won't need to worry about what happens here, although in his mind he still sits thinking of how ridiculous the thought of a portal to another world really is, it has to be earth, just because he doesn't recognise the plants and trees means nothing, he's never been to the amazon or any of the remote areas on this planet that could hold such life, but regardless even being able to go the amazon would be pretty fucking cool and maybe just maybe he can try to understand how the rock works, whether he can harness the rock to provide portals to other places. As he's sitting thinking of all the possibilities, he starts to feel the tiredness sweep over him again and closes his laptop, sitting back and finishing his drink he sits back to get some sleep.

    5am the next morning he's woken by a knock on the door and a female handing him a cup of coffee "We will be ready to leave on time make sure you have everything this is a one-way trip and deliveries are difficult in Siberia" at that she turns on her heels and locks the door again. Left on his own again holding his coffee one thing keeps coming to his mind "This is a one-way trip" what the hell did she mean by that? Although he's pretty sure she meant exactly what she said, this is Russia after all and as far as they are concerned the bunker doesn't exist and by default that would mean the people at the bunker do not exist either. Pacing the room waiting for the door to be unlocked again, drinking his coffee it all hits him again, this really is it, no way to back out and no way to ensure he can leave if this doesn't work, everything is hinged on him being able to leave another way, after all as Petrov said, he no longer exists.

CHAPTER 17

Like clockwork bang on 6am the door is unlocked and swings open, the same female that bought him his morning coffee hands him a coat "You will need this where we are going" looking at the coat it will certainly keep him warmer than the one he has, putting it on and zipping it up she turns on her heels again "Follow me", not exactly the most talkative guide. Walking out of the room toward the back entrance again, he's led to another black Mercedes, climbing in the back seat she shuts the door and gets in the driver's seat. As they start to pull out of the car park she finally speaks a little more "I am Nikita I'll be your liaison from here on Petrov has a lot of information to go through thanks to you if you need anything when you're at the bunker there is a secure messaging linked only to me I will be the only person you will see today until we arrive at the bunker for safety reasons of course" Alex simply looks into the rear view mirror and nods, then settles down to look out of the window, sitting thinking how much he would have liked to be able to look around Moscow, he's never been but the architecture is amazing, but this isn't that kind of trip.

Half an hour later they slow and pull into a private airport, with one plane sat on the runway and no else to be seen, as they pull up alongside the private jet Nikita walks round and opens his door and walks him up the stairs on to the plane, as he sits down Nikita shows him the drinks fridge, it's not even 7am but as far as Alex is concerned now, he is on flexy time. Just as he starts to wonder who's flying the plane Nikita walks off and heads for the cockpit, I guess at least he knows who his pilot is now and why she said she would be the only person he will see until they arrive at the bunker. As the engines start the PA system starts "We will arrive at another private airport in around two hours the weather is clear once we land it will take another hour to get to the bunker, I suggest you enjoy a drink and some music any requests?" straight away he asks for Shinedown and music kicks in, all he can do for now is sit back and enjoy some music and whisky, who cares if it's 7am he doesn't exist right?

Looking out of the window, city turns to farm land, farm land turns to forest and forest turns to snow and for once he's so taken with the scenery that at least for now his mind has gone quiet, apart from the one bump in the flight, a slight bit of turbulence that almost makes him thrown whisky in his own face, the flight goes by pretty smoothly and he managed to avoid spilling his whisky. Just under two hours later the seatbelt light pings on and they start their descent, looking out of the window he can see nothing apart from a watch tower and a single runway, no roads or anything leading away from the airport, so now is just to wait and see how they will travel the last stretch of the journey to the bunker. As the plane touches down and slows to a stop, the engines slow and eventually stop and Nikita comes walking back through to the cabin "We are here from here there is an underground system that goes directly into the bunker you will go alone and once at the bunker the train will come back here" following Nikita down the steps of the plane she leads him over to watch tower, as they walk over he realises why he needed a thicker coat, the temperature is now about -20c "I'll never complain about Scottish weather again" nothing from Nikita not even a twitch. As they approach the door, that has quite a modern key pad to unlock it, considering the age and remoteness of the airstrip. Nikita carefully covers her hand so as not to give away the pin and doors opens slowly, she points to a ladder in the centre and sends Alex on his way, down the ladder he gets to a small platform, with what looks like an old London tube train sitting waiting, as he steps on and sits down the doors close and the train departs, all he can assume is that it runs remotely, so for the next hour he'll be sat hurtling underground through Siberia until he gets to the bunker.

After a while the hum of the train and the flashing lights coming from the tunnel start to affect his eyes and ears, the constant flash of bright light, fading then flashing over and over again starts to feel like his eyes are burning, the only thing he can do for now is close his eyes and sit back and wait for the journey to end. Eventually after what seems like about 3 hours the train finally starts drawing to a stop, opening his eyes and looking out of the single carriage train window he sees a small station that reminds him more of grand central station in New York, with its ornate carvings, tall ceiling and gold paintwork. Leaving the train, he starts to wonder why they would have built something so elaborate in the middle of Siberia? For now he looks around for something to sit on to at least try to get his bearings back and let his eyesight readjust, spotting a single bench by the wall, he sits down rubbing his eyes as a gentle tap on the shoulder makes him jump "What the fuck?" a gentle female voice behind him apologizes in a Russian accent, standing up he turns to see a woman in her early 30's, small build with the giveaway nerds glasses "You must be Alexander" he looks almost like he's seen a ghost, only one person ever called him Alexander and that was him mum "Alex please just Alex" a little smile "Alex follow me I'm Oksana" the pair walk to the end of the platform to what looks like an ancient goods lift, that certainly doesn't fit in with the rest of the station aesthetics "The rest are eager to meet you you're the first new person outside of our group we have seen for 5 years" As Oksana punches the single button on the lifts panel he starts to wonder what sort of set up this is, no one new for 5 years? That doesn't sound right and also doesn't sound like any sort of job he's ever heard of "5 years? Do you ever leave?" She just shakes her head a little "We will explain once we're all sat together but you may wish you never came"

CHAPTER 18

As the lift jolts to a stop Oksana slides the metal door to the side opening it up to white painted concrete warehouse space that looks a million miles away from the lavish train station, which he is now considering moving into if this is what the rest of the bunker looks like, looking around not saying a word everything suddenly hits him, this is his life now unless they find another way out. Oksana reaches out and taps his shoulder, the recoil from it almost made him fall over, which Oksana finds highly amusing "Everybody reacts that way or at least we did when we arrived here" Alex still trying to process everything turns to Oksana "How long have you been here?" Oksana shrugs and leads him through a side door into a small slightly better decorated dining room, as he walks in, he suddenly sees another 15 sets of eyes looking straight at him, every single one of them look like they haven't seen another person other than the group for years. Oksana leaves him standing by the door and goes to take a seat towards the far end of the table, leaving the seat at the end of the table closest to

Alex empty, as Alex takes his seat a red-haired woman at the other end of the table stands up "I am Nikita Romanov kind of I guess a leader here your arrival has been a bit of a surprise to us we found out this morning that you were coming although we have no idea why anyone would volunteer to come here of their own free will we as a team have been here for almost 8 years and we know from the history of this place we won't be leaving alive and whether you realise it or not neither will you unless you have made arrangements with Petrov which I doubt" Alex sits looking at the table trying to process what Nikita has just said "But what about the train?" a question that the rest of the team seem to find amusing "That train comes here and always leaves empty one person has attempted the return journey only to be shot when he got to Moscow and the rest of us lost what few privileges we have for a month because we allowed him to try you can ask us any questions you have if you only answer one of ours" Alex looks up and nods as Nikita asks the one question he knew was coming "Why did you come here?" Alex takes the chance to stand up "OK so you've already opened my eyes I knew coming here was a risk but what I'm here to do isn't something easily explained and is probably better to show you once I have found a space to work but I need to ask about surveillance here" one of the men answer this "The only place we are not monitored is in our bedrooms everywhere else has cameras and mics"

That was all Alex needed a means to talk privately "OK for now I'm quite tired from all the travelling I am going to have a short sleep if someone could show me my room" Nikita instantly takes the lead and shows him the way through.

As they leave the room and walk down a small corridor with rooms leading off left and right she shows him to the end room, the only empty room in the base "This was Michaels room until he tried the train journey to Moscow" walking in and signalling for Nikita to follow he shuts the door behind her and in a low voice speaks freely "I may have a way for all of us to leave here but I need a way to show you that won't be seen or heard by anyone in Moscow well anyone anywhere outside of this bunker" Nikita looking puzzled

"We are only here to run the nuclear power it's the one job we were all trained for we are all orphans and outside of this bunker we have nothing"

"I may be able to offer you more but I need to work out a way of doing some tests without being seen"

"That may prove difficult but as for a way of speaking to us without being heard or seen we have a weekly poker night that is exempt from the normal rules the one night we are allowed to gather in one room away from cameras and that is tonight so this is the only night for a week you will be able to get all of us together in private and also there will be plenty of vodka"

"I can't say I'm very good at poker but I am good at vodka if you would agree to me coming with you"

"You are here that makes you part of the team whether your here to work with us or not you have been outside of this place we have no idea what has been happening for 8 years and if you can truly offer us freedom we will listen"

Both of them spin around at a knock on the door which Nikita opens "Ah Pasha you have our guests luggage" Pasha walks in and places Alex's two bags down and turns and walks out" Nikita lets out a small laugh "Pasha isn't the most talkative person until he gets some vodka in him tonight you won't be able to shut him up now I need to leave you here and get the team back to work before we have a meltdown" Nikita leaves but that last statement gives him and idea, if his plan does work and right now that is a big if since he has no way of testing what power he will need if he can't disable some cameras and mics, but he could use the reactor as a way to stop them following, at least for a start, but they have a direct route using the train, this is going to take some planning and a shit load of dumb luck to pull off and he still doesn't know if he can even do it and survive but for now, although he was lying about being tired so that he could talk privately, he needs an hour to get over the shock of being here and being told he just gave himself a life sentence until they can truly use that damn rock to get out of here, starting to feel angry at his parents for putting him in this situation, he lays down on the bed not even taking his shoes off and closes his eyes.

8pm that night a knock on the door wakes him up "Alex poker night" Nikita pushes the door open "Are you coming? You've been asleep for hours" rubbing his eyes Alex slides his phone into his pocket and follows Nikita into one of the other rooms, looking around he smiles at the various trinkets around the room and the table with 17 glasses and a bottle of vodka in the middle, this must be the biggest room since there is space for all of them to gather around the table. Another one of the men talk to this "I'm Mitya this is the one night of the week we all live for and just as a warning we usually don't sleep till the very early hours but here we can talk freely without persecution" Alex smiles "I'm glad about that I'm sure you all have questions and I do too" at that it's Pasha this time "What has been happening out there we haven't heard anything for years" Alex laughs what's been happening for 8 years that's a hard one to answer in one night I guess the main thing that would matter to all of you is that Vladimir Putin has launched an attack on the Ukraine seeming he wants the old soviet back as it was either that or he is mentally ill" They all stare at Alex in disbelief "So even if we were to leave here we would be at war sounds like we die here or we die out there" Nikita next "What Pasha says sounds right we die anyway you mentioned something earlier could you explain?" She grabs the vodka bottle and starts pouring drinks for everyone "OK I haven't had chance to work out all of the ins and outs of a plan yet but my parents left me a task before they died and from what I have been able to do so far I might have a way for all of us to leave it's hard to explain but I have a photo I'd like your opinions about" Picking up his glass and downing his vodka in one go he opens up the photo on his phone and passes it to Pasha first" Pasha look goes from shock to confusion to excited as he passes the phone around the table "Where is that?" Alex pours himself a second vodka "That's part of the problem I don't know at the moment where it is but if you could all look a little closer at the plant life and surrounding areas of the photo it might help us all understand" the room falls silent as the phone goes around the table, people zooming in and out trying to look at everything, then the whispers in Russian so Alex can't understand as he sits quietly sipping at his vodka leaving them to discuss everything.

Another one the men stand "I don't know where that is it certainly isn't anywhere; we would know most of us were in our teens when we were sent here, I will try to explain our background a little since it's the same for all of us. We are all orphans or at least as far as we know we are, we were taken by the Russian government officials as children most of us were living on the streets and we were taken to a Russian academy the only way any of us leave that place is either in a body bag or to somewhere like this we have no life we lived better on the streets so I'm going to say this, if you have a way for us to leave this hell I will follow even if I get killed by Russia or whatever I would like to feel some freedom before I die" at that Sacha sits down again, to large banging on the table of glasses apparently in approval. With a smile Nikita quiets the banging on the table "Well I guess you have us all on board what do you need?" That is a difficult one for Alex "That's the problem I need two things, privacy and power and it would seem I can't have both at the same time" The bang of a glass on the table and a thick Russian accent blurts out "That I can do but only a short time maybe 30 minutes" Alex looks across the table at the older looking member of the team, a rugged looking man with a scar running down the left of his face who Nikita announces as Lazar "If that's all I can get I will work with that" and Lazar nods "Tomorrow I will give you a tour and show you where I can do it" Then a bellowing but joyful voice "Deal the damn cards" and that would be Igor proudly announces Lazar "The chemist of the group"

As the night goes on and Alex starts learning the rules of poker, badly but learning the team talk freely and some sort of plan starts to come together, they discuss what they can and can't take, being without any sort of vehicle apart from a fork lift truck proves to be a point of contention mainly because a fork lift truck would be risky to take through and probably just block up the cave and make it all harder for them, so everything has to be carried, which means stock piling what they need in view of the cameras and they have one night to plan it unless they want to wait a week. As everyone starts to get tired and draw the nights poker to an end, they have worked out much of the plan, what to take, who's taking what and where to gather everything and best place to set everything up. The main warehouse area is usually used to gather equipment that is either broken or no longer needed to return on a train once a fortnight and since the train only came in the day before Alex arrived it isn't due for another two weeks, so that is where it will all happen, hopefully. The only thing that is troubling Alex is will they survive, none of them know anything about survival in the wild, the team haven't even had freedom since they were taken as children, but as it has been bluntly said time and time again, no one leaves this place alive.

CHAPTER 19

As everybody slowly starts to wake up, some with hangovers, all with questions they can't ask until either next week or after it's too late, Alex is already sat in the dining room with a coffee when the first member turns up with an obvious headache, Lubov makes herself a black coffee and sits with her head in her hands "Every week I say no more hangovers every fucking week I wake up feeling like I've been hit by a sledge hammer" Alex can't help but laugh "sorry I don't mean to be rude" looking through her fingers "If it didn't hurt I'd be laughing too" The next to come through is a slightly more upbeat and apparently not as hungover is Lazar "I will have a coffee my friend and we will have a tour just let me know when you're ready you may want a pen and paper to write down where things are" Taking the hint Alex finishes his coffee and goes to get his small bag and pen and paper and walks back through, noticing Lazar has barely touched his coffee he takes the opportunity to make another, as he sits Lazar slides him a piece of paper "Here is a map for you" Looking at the paper, no map just a message but they are obviously pros at hiding things here, scrawled on the paper is a simple message "Don't talk just follow my lead"

Looking around the dining area properly for the first time, the walls are plastered with posters that are supposed to look nice but are all Russian propaganda material, the funny part of this is that almost all of them have some mention or imagery about freedom, a freedom that for these people doesn't exist, apart from that the walls are covered in pale blues and yellows, probably to make it feel warmer as a communal area, but for Alex he can't help but think of the Ukraine, yet another misdirection in the room, it soon becomes apparent that everything in this room is a contradiction. Finishing his coffee Lazar stands up "Ready Alex?" Alex leaves what's left in his cup and follows Lazar back in to the warehouse area, as Lazar points out different areas, especially the steel doors on the right side of the room, covered in warning signs "That is the way in to the main power plant I would recommend you stay away from there for your own safety" Alex nods making notes as they walk around. Walking a little further they arrive near the end of the room, having a quick look around Alex can see one single camera which Lazar stands directly under and signals to Alex to follow, scribbling a note on Alex's notepad "I can give this camera a quick power overload it usually takes them around 45 minutes to repair remotely do you have what you need?" Taking the pad back "Is there a strong power supply here? I want you to see this so you can tell the others" Lazar nods and points at two wires on the ground and a small panel on the wall, a test area, although not quite what Alex expected once last note from Alex "How old is this place? Are you ready?" Lazar picks up the wires and nods before scribbling one last note before he disables the camera "Pre second world war" Touching the red wire to the base of the camera then carefully the second wire and the light on the camera suddenly goes out with a nod from Lazar.

Alex immediately snaps into action not wanting to waste time he has something he wants to test, not able to risk bringing the drone through with him for fear of it being heard or seen by Moscow, pulling the foil lined bag out with the rock inside he makes sure the power is off before he unwraps it. Placing it down on the floor he turns to Lazar, who is looking as confused as a child being told he can have as many sweets as he wants, Alex just smiles and takes the rock from its bag, pacing a cable either side of it. Pressing the light on the panel and putting the power level just over what he used before, wanting to generate a slightly bigger portal. As soon as he punches the green panel the rock does its spin, quicker than before maybe because of the extra power, Lazar struggles to stay quiet holding his hands to his mouth as the rock raises, spinning quicker and quicker. There is only one thing Alex wants from this and as the black orb rises slightly from the top of the rock and starts opening out, as soon as it gets large enough for Alex to walk through, he holds a hand up to tell lazar to stay where he is, looking at Lazar his face is a funny shade of grey right now. Making sure Lazar understood Alex takes a small step forward, being this close to it he starts hearing a slight pulsing hum, then taking a deep breath he takes another step forward watching as his foot goes through the portal as he places it on the cave floor, but this isn't same cave he saw last time, maybe the change in location affects where the portal opens and it's just pure dumb luck that it's another cave. Leaning forward slightly he puts a hand through, noticing a distinct change in temperature, cool but not too cold, which is reassuring as he would have liked to test this more before he risked going through, but he doesn't have that luxury anymore. Taking another deep breath and holding it he steps all the way through, the first thing he notices is the air is cleaner, no fumes, nothing that he can smell apart from plant life, the temperature seems nice and he has no odd feelings, time for the main test, he exhales and tries to breath and almost jumps in the air when he can, looking behind him through the portal Lazar is now sat on the floor looking like he's in prayer, as Alex takes a few steps he can notice a difference, a small gravity difference, gravity is lighter here but not much but it should actually aid them. At that he decides he should probably go back just in case anything goes wrong, stepping back through the portal he realises just how much things smell back in the bunker. Alex didn't realise the huge grin on his face as Lazar mutters something in Russian followed by "Are you ok? What the fuck is that?" Alex laughing a little "That's our way to freedom and now I know more, it's safe and it's not Russia" Lazar looking even more perplexed signals him to put the rock away then scribbles a note, remembering himself they can't talk freely "Said too much already I don't care where it is we.re going through that thing tomorrow if the rest are ready let's get a vodka" Packing the rock back up as Lazar scribbles a note for the rest of the team the two of them start the walk back to the dining room.

Walking back through the door, everybody is there and everybody is looking as Lazar disappears to the kitchen and comes back with two glasses of vodka, taking the notepad and handing it round "Look at how bad his map is" as the team read the note, a deadly silence falls among the group and the realisation that this is it, this is freedom or at least it will be the best chance they have, the notepad makes it back round to Alex, on scribbled question "Earth?" he sits and ponders his answer for a minute then shakes his head, he knows now that it isn't and the look from the rest of the group is something between excitement and horror. Lazar is making a note for the group again and double checks it with Alex before passing it around

Collect as much equipment, food and drink as you can carry this is a one-way trip no returns if you don't want to come, you're on your own

I'm blowing the reactor on the way out as security

As the note is passed around everybody nods in agreement and gets up to go to their jobs for one last day Alex heads back to his room with his bag to have a look through his own notes, mindful not to take long, not wanting to trigger any calls from Petrov although his first full day at the bunker he probably wouldn't be missed much, but just to make sure he has a quick scan through his notes and heads back to the dining room for another coffee before he goes for a look around, although he has one plan for the morning, he's taking some war memorabilia with him from that little room to the side of the warehouse. Taking his coffee with him he heads through to the main warehouse area.

Starting on the right side of the room he takes a slow walk around, the warehouse is probably bigger than a football stadium and pretty much empty, if the warehouse is this big how big is the reactor and how safe can a prewar reactor really be? And more importantly what is it for? It makes no sense that a reactor would be built this far into complete isolation and be a protected secret, walking a little further up he pushes an unlocked door open expecting to see some sort of store room or equipment room, but when he turns on the light, he stands staring at a war room, with an old soviet map still pinned to the wall, this was a backup, if everything went wrong this is where the command centre was going to be, it has to be it's the only explanation for the reactor and the war room, closing the door he keeps following the left side, one more room down here, pushing the door open to see a room full of equipment, something he was expecting to see and hoping to find, walking in looking at the tools and other bits, he needs to get a bag in here so he collect what he wants, then pick it up in the morning.

Walking back out of the room and looking around, the only thing on this side is the corner where he tested the portal, the camera is back on but he doesn't care now, on the opposite side is just the main door for the reactor. Finding himself at a loose end and with it only just coming up to mid-day he takes a walk back to the dining room, missing the fact that the rest of the team are taking it in turns to start gathering stuff together, desperately trying not to gain any attention from cameras and mics, As Alex settles down with his notepad he starts to wonder just how isolated they must feel here, unable to talk openly except for one night a week, unable to stand outside, no freedom or sense of anything other than this concrete bunker.

CHAPTER 20

Bang on 5pm the door to the dining area swings open, with a much happier crowd than the one that left the dining room at 9am, Nikita stands in front of one camera and makes what looks like a secret sign and waits, then a small flash of light comes from below the light and in Russian she asks a question and waits again, a double flash from the camera's light and they all bang the table in unison "What the hell was that?" Nikita laughs "Poker night again" Alex smiles glad to be able to talk freely again, passing notes around all day feels more like he should be working as a Russian spy than a visitor to a secret bunker with a huge reactor in it, the only reason he knew about it was a rumour online that was wiped from existence as quick as it went up, only caught by a handful of people one of the being the late friend of Alex, John Duncan.

For now, one of the women, he hasn't been introduced to rushes to the kitchen to quickly prepare some food, which seems to take about 10 minutes, nothing fabulous but it's edible and everyone eats at top speed, obviously wanting to get some privacy as soon as possible, finishing they're food in what looks like record time they all get up leaving Alex still eating "Come through for poker once you're finished snail" they all walk off laughing. Alex finishes his food as quick as he can, which is slow, he's been a slow eater, but this food would probably be better rushed and then washed down with vodka, so he understands why they eat so fast. Getting up and heading straight for the door, he can hear them clearly as he walks through into the corridor, walking into the room Lazar passes him a vodka "We have muffled the mics for tonight so here's to freedom" everybody raises they're glasses.

Alex sits down as Nikita speaks "We have gathered as much as we can we all have a bag ready Lazar has made sure we have enough vodka until his chemistry set can brew some more and we've rigged the reactor to blow just a push of a button and the coolant will be cut off, a small charge has been set to disable any outside interference Lazar told us about the rock and I hope we're not leaving it here?" Alex shakes his head "Not a chance it has to come with us for our own safety I don't know what we will meet when we get there but it's up to us as a group to forge a new life after this and you can all gain a freedom you've never known at least if we die there it's in our hands and no one else is every one coming?" That same large bang of glasses answers that question as in unison they down they're vodkas.

All Alex can hope for at this point is that they can somehow work out how to survive with nothing but what they can carry and as a team and not separate, most of his fears have calmed down or at least his fears for this part, what awaits them tomorrow is anyone's guess right now, he hasn't seen any animals or life apart from plants and he hasn't had time to do any of the research he would have liked to but he has no way of changing that now. He still stands by his decision not to talk to anyone but the Russians, had he have approached the UK government they would have asked too many questions and wanted control of everything and would have probably not included him in anything, at least with the Russians he could pay them in a way that would keep them quiet, although surveillance at the bunker is high, they've all found ways around that and done it as one, which gives him a little hope that they can do this. Can they really do this?

For the rest of the night the mood stays high and the vodka keeps flowing although Lubov seems to be drinking a little more conservatively tonight obviously not wanting to end up in the same state she was in this morning, Alex spends the night telling them about the last 8 years in the world, especially about the war in the Ukraine, which filled them with horror and made them glad to be leaving this behind, some of them it turns out are actually Ukrainian although they have no real memories of the Ukraine and little loyalty to any country it seems. As the story starts to go onto how Alex came across the piece of rock, they almost seem to be listening to a story like a bunch of kids listening to a story about grand adventures, which I guess in some ways this could be, but it certainly isn't for children. Explaining about the death of his old colleague John on Petrov's orders and his two American acquaintances they all ah and gasp in the right places, as the story moves forward, they ask how he was allowed to come here with no questions asked, a question that he'd been dreading, not sure how it would be greeted and for it come this close to D-Day isn't something he relished. Taking a deep breath, he goes into the details of using information to gain access, which it seems is something they agree with, but then they have been groomed by Russians so that should probably be no surprise. Alex for some reason decides to pull his phone out wanting to check the news, since he's actively avoided checking any news since handing the information to the Russians. Hiding his phone under the table and checking the news the first thing he sees is that Russia has with no reason pulled their astronauts from the ISS, not something he expected to see so soon but also something he knew would be happening at some point, this information he decides to keep to himself for the time being not wanting to unveil any other surprises so close to what's happening in the morning.

As the poker continues and the stories start to run down, they decide around 3am to call it a night ready for the morning, the plan is for them to continue as normal or at least act as normal as possible but they won't need to act for long, Lazar has made sure the plant will go into meltdown and the rest of them have gathered everything they could, as soon as they go to work Alex will pack what he wants to take and bang on 10am they leave so Alex needs to make sure everything is ready, including securing the rock to pull through when they are all through, for that he has two chains, one attached to a hook so it can turn freely without snagging as the rock spins and a smaller one that will be secured around the rock hanging from the chain, hopefully that's enough because they will see what they did and they will see them leave.

As everybody leaves the room, they all slap Alex on the back on the way past, which after sixteenth person starts to hurt a little, but he doesn't complain. He doesn't even know half of their names yet, but there's plenty of time for that when this is done. Alex heads to his own room, tired but happy. He still can't quite believe their doing this, thankfully he hasn't had time to think too much about it, because no matter how determined he might be when he sets his mind to something he knows he would have backed out of it had he thought too much about it. Climbing into bed with an alarm for 8am, it doesn't take long to fall asleep and as soon as his alarm goes office jumps up to the sound of voices in the corridor, the rest of the team are going or coffee, he'd better get moving, he won't get much coffee after this for a while.

Walking through to the dining room, there's smiles but it's business as usual for now, they all have their coffee and bang on 9am they make their way through to the reactor, which he asked about the size last night and all he was told is bigger than anything else they know of. 9am it's time to get this plan moving, they have all left so Alex heads to his room grabbing two bags one containing the rock and the biggest bag he has for everything else, not wasting time he heads straight back out and towards the store room, when he walks in the first thing he sees is 15 bags lined up ready to go, packing everything he put to one side, he heads to the corner of the warehouse, checking the time it's now almost 9.50am, 10 minutes to go. Just at that point he hears a loud bang coming from the reactor area and the rest start a quick walk over. Pulling the rock from its bag still contained in the foil bag he places it down, looking over his shoulder to make sure the power is off, just as he reaches for the zip on the foil lined bag his phone pings, there is only one person who even knows he has this phone, Petrov "Alex I don't know what you're doing but I recommend you stop right now" putting his phone away and ignoring Petrov, he slips the rock out and carefully attaches the chains "OK I'm ready if you are" everyone nods, bags over their shoulders "I'll go last" as Alex starts to pull the wires over, then puts the power up high, at punches the green button for the last time, the rock lifts and spins to a set of gasps from everyone else "Go now" as soon as the portal open they make their way through as quick as they can, just as Alex gets through and tugs at the chain a hand comes around the side of him trying to reach back through for a note on the floor, Alex screams for the to pull back but it's too late, just as the rock comes through on the chain and portal closes in a flash, Pasha's arms slips through and portal immediately cuts it off just below the elbow.

Pasha collapses at Alex's feet, blood pouring out over the cave floor, as Alex looks down, he has to stop himself panicking at the sight of Pasha's bone, muscle and tendons showing, composing himself he quietly calls for Nikita, Sacha follows Nikita as Alex moves away to let them in. Looking at the rest of the group, most of them are crying and white as a sheet, Alex thinks quickly wanting to distract everyone from Pasha as much as he can "Let's go and have a look outside, we can't stay here for long" Alex starts walking past everyone toward the cave entrance, keeping an eye out for any markings, praying there is none, the team are already struggling he'd rather not address the fact that there is or has been someone else here, on the way past the bags he notices a Geiger counter and picks it up, turning it on, he starts to realise this would have been wiser to do before he brought the whole group through, looking at the reading, breathing a sign of relief when he see's the reading 15cpm, a safe level. Walking to the entrance the rest have fallen in line behind him, all apprehensive and most of them should have probably bought clean underwear with them, they might need it. Standing at the entrance they find themselves staring out at what looks like a thick jungle, the ground is moist and covered in foliage, flowers of dark reds and purples, the trees are thicker and taller than earths, even making giant redwoods look like normal trees, 15 sets of eyes looking all around, the planet looks untouched and beautiful, no roads or overhead wires, the air is fresh and there isn't a bunker in sight, at least if they die here they die free from the shackles that Russia put them in. Looking up at the forest roof, Alex can see the moon clearly through a gap in leaves, a huge natural satellite with a slight red tint, almost pink. Alex stands in his own thoughts trying to remember what would cause the red tint, the only thing that comes to mind is the star in this system is a red dwarf.

The first one to talk is Lazar, a short man, bald with bright blue eyes, eyes that are currently looking in every direction, trying to take everything in "Alex where is this? Do you have any idea?" Looking round at Lazar trying to think of anywhere he can think of that would even come close, Alex shrugs "I'm not sure maybe Trappist but honestly I have no idea" Lazar just looks confused and why not he hasn't seen the sun or anything for 5 years, none of them have. The group look like kids who have been let loose in a sweet shop, as Alex steps out of the cave, with Lazar closely behind him, he suddenly jumps as the whole forest floor seems to come to life around him, small animals scatter and run away, some of the flowers quickly close up, almost in protection, looking up through the trees, leaves of dark greens, reds and purples, lit only by the glow of the moon. Alex turns almost jumping as he ends up nose to nose with Lazar, who was so close behind him he could have been wearing his shoes, looking around at the group "OK if you want to have a look around you can but stay in a group for safety, I'm going to check on Pasha and come up with a plan" Alex walks past the group suddenly feeling like a primary school teacher, hold hands so you don't get lost kiddies.

As he gets close to Nikita, he looks down to see Pasha wide eyed in shock, Sacha stands up, still looking white as a ghost "He'll be OK as long as we can keep the wound clean and avoid infection, Nikita found a blow torch in a bag and cauterized the wound, but he's in shock he didn't react to the pain so we need to be careful" Alex kneels down in front of Pasha, who is looking directly at him, but it feels like he's looking through him "Sacha could you stay with him while me and Nikita come up with a plan?" Sacha nods and sits on a rock at the side of Pasha as Alex and Nikita move away, looking at Nikita all he can see is fear and blood stained clothes and hands and then suddenly for the first time, the fiery redhead starts to cry, leaning on Alex with her head on his shoulder. For the first time he has seen Nikita look vulnerable, in the bunker she was always in charge and never wavered, now, he can see the softer side of her. Leading her to the cave entrance and rolling two small rocks over they sit looking out at the rest of the group, quietly looking around, touching plants and flowers and oddly enough some of them are smiling, a look of pure emotion, something Alex can never remember a time he's seen it.

Sitting looking outside Nikita rests her head on Alex's shoulder, with Alex trying to not to make too much of it "What do we do now Alex?"
"I never thought that far ahead I guess I never thought we'd make it this far"
"We can't really move Pasha yet so maybe we

should stay in the cave until morning?"
"This cave isn't the one we saw in the portal before the forest is thicker here and…. Shit"
"And what?"
"Nothing it doesn't matter"
"Now is not the time for secrets Alex"
"In the photo of the cave I had on my phone there was a marking on the wall by the entrance, a petroglyph I'm sorry I just didn't want the whole group worrying or worse"
"You should have said, from now on no secrets even if you only tell me, who do you think it is?"
"I have no idea they might not even be here now"
"I'll tell the group when things have calmed down for now I think we should call the group back and organise a scouting mission find out what we have around us"
"Agreed and thank you I could take Lazar out with me while you organise the others and watch Pasha, but we'll wait till morning"
"Sounds like a plan I'll tell them there may be others here I'll say we might have found tracks"
"Do you think they'll be OK with that?"
"They'll have to be they need to know"
"OK I'll go tell Lazar you're the boss when we go"
"Fuck off pig I am no boss"
"They look at you like the boss"
"Part of my job at the bunker was to keep them in line I'm the only one that wasn't an orphan I was

taken from my family I understood a little more than they did"

"I'm sorry I can't imagine what you've all been through"

"We'll talk about it later"

Standing up and walking back into the cave Alex takes a look at Pasha, who is still staring into space, a sign that doesn't look promising to Alex but he's no doctor. Walking over to Lazar who is looking through bags Alex explains the plan, thinking Lazar would try to refuse, instead Lazar jumps up ready to explore their new home, then sun has started to rise so the pair head out of the cave passing Nikita on the way, Alex gently squeezes her shoulder on the way, walking out into the open Alex can finally see why everyone was so happy, the forest is beautiful, not one sign of deforestation or pollution, all of the things that are wrong with earth. As they walk through the trees attention turns to looking for anything moving, which at the moment seems to be everything, every other step, something scuttles away or a twig breaks, but so far they haven't seen anything, the forest is too thick to see much beyond a tree's distance, only walking in one direction to avoid getting lost, but still hoping they don't get turned around and end up lost anyway. A few more minutes Alex stops Lazar

"Wait I think for now we should head back to the cave and maybe get some string or something to mark our route I don't like how thick this forest is and we can't afford to get lost" Turning around it's Lazar who finally works out which way they came by looking for broken twigs, things look different on the way back, Alex has already seen a marking or possibly a marking on a tree, a red line, waist height, showing Lazar who says nothing just looks and carries on walking. Getting past a few more trees, almost back at the cave Lazar stops dead with one hand on a tree, Alex pulls his hand away to see a triangle with a circle in the middle carved then painted on a tree, no denying or hiding it now, they are not alone here and whoever is here has some intelligence, now they just need to know how much and where they are.

As they get close enough to the cave to see the entrance, Lazar finally cracks a smile, most of the group are working on constructing a wall and a door to seal the cave entrance and at least act as some sort of safe shelter at least for now until they can work out a better plan. Lazar gets straight to helping with the wall while Alex goes to the back of the cave to check on Nikita, Sacha and Pasha "How is he?" Alex jumps back when Pasha grabs his leg "He's alive" Alex smiles and kneels down, other than a missing left arm Pasha seems in surprisingly good spirits. Alex stands back up and goes to help finish off the wall and door, the cave is big enough for now, but not for long, as soon as they are safe they need to start thinking of plans and Alex needs to know who he's with, everything happened so fast he still hasn't even got names for everybody and has barely spoken to anyone but Lazar, Nikita and Sacha, so working out how they survive together could take time.

CHAPTER 21

As soon as the cave entrance is sealed and a door is in place the group sit down in a circle around Pasha, who is now propped up against the cave wall, a little more colour in his face and he's talking which is at least an improvement. As Alex joins in the conversation the subject goes to what happened in the past, mainly the academy, the reason they all ended in being given a life sentence in a secret bunker with no one to miss them and no one even knowing about them. Plucked from the streets as orphans, all apart from Nikita who was taken from her parents, apparently the Russians like to keep tabs on the schools and any child that shows the sort of intelligence they are looking for mysteriously disappears, sent to the academy to be brain washed and trained by the Kremlin, subjects depended on what they need in the future, nuclear sciences is a top one it would seem, that and nuclear warfare, which Pasha was almost taken into but it turns out he liked to ask questions and wasn't great at taking orders, which is shown by the scars when he lifts his top a little to show what happens when you don't conform. A couple of hours talking as a group and Alex starts to learn just how much they have been hidden from, they know barely anything of the outside world and what's been happening, Alex has been filling in bits here and there but it's hard to know what to tell them or even how to tell them about the last 40 years let alone all the history they know nothing about.

Alex stands and takes a walk to the cave entrance, opening the door slightly to take a look outside, there's a lot more noise coming from the forest now and the light is dimming, which makes Alex pull a small notepad from his pocket and jot down the time on his watch to at least try and work out the length of the days and sunset, sunrise times, 7pm sunset seems relatively normal. Closing the door he heads back to the group "The suns setting so for tonight I think we should stay in the cave, no wandering around we don't know what's out there" It's Rada that speaks next, a quiet 38 year old who is going grey early "Or who, why didn't you just tell us?" Alex shuffles a little feeling more than a little uncomfortable "I guess I didn't know any of you and I didn't know how the news would impact you but from now on no secrets I promise" Rada nods in acknowledgement and leaves it at that, with Alex not sure what that means or how the rest feel about the news.

CHAPTER 22

As the evening turns to night and things outside seem quiet Alex gets up having remained quiet for much of the evening, mainly due to not being sure how the news of not being alone here went and most of the group talking among themselves in Russian. Walking to the piles of bags at the back of the cave, the first thing he does is place the rock back in its case for safety and grabs three bottles of vodka, since someone in the group, who he can probably narrow down to one, Lazar decided it would be good to bring as much as he can, just as he turns to walk back there is huge screeching noise from outside. The entire group fall silent all looking around at each other, then to the cave entrance thankful they can't see what made the noise, at least for now. As Alex walks over still holding the camera case containing the rock, there's another huge screech followed by a low rumbling growl, then Alex has a thought and slowly unzips the camera case. As soon as the case is open again, they hear shuffling outside, getting quieter, the animals are backing off, Alex sits with the group and takes a mouthful of vodka and passes the bottles around, signalling for everyone to be quiet as he zips the case up again. The second it's closed again the animals come back to the cave entrance in number, what sounds like at least 10 now outside the make shift wall, making Alex jump and unzip the case immediately, whatever is out there is either afraid of the rock or knows something they don't, but for the night Alex decides it stays out in the open, everyone feels safer that way and slowly the conversations start again this time in English so Alex can take part, with the group accepting that they are not alone and Akex was just trying to avoid worrying them.

Now the conversations have changed to talk about what is outside and why the rock has so much importance to the animals out there, Lazar gets up to stretch his legs and notices the blue glints in the cave wall, and grabs a knife to see if he can pry a piece from the wall to study, managing to get a small piece he walks back over and drops it into an empty can and sets it down on the fire, leaving it there for a bit to see what happens with the group almost oblivious, partly through tiredness, mainly through vodka. Alex moves round to sit by Lazar as some of the group start to fall asleep after Alex tells them he and Lazar will take first watch. Lazar picks the can up from the fire looking into it confused, Alex takes it and looks just as puzzled the blue material is metallic and has a very low melting point. Tipping the can up expecting the metal to have welded itself to the can, it just drops out on to the cave floor, Lazar reaches forward and picks it up, it's cool already which makes handling it easier, with it being free from the rock that was stuck to it he can finally see properly what it is. Blue metal that feels more solid than its melting point would suggest. Passing it to Alex who studies it for a minute before placing it down on a rock and picking up another rock, smashing it down expecting it to either break apart or change shape, he was shocked by what happened as the rock broke in two in his hands with no effect at all on the metal. Turning to the Lazar who is looking very happy with himself at the moment "This could be useful it's everywhere in here if we can make moulds for tools and parts we'll be able to make what we need to survive" Lazar claps him on the shoulder "Small victories my friend"

Alex goes back to sit on his rock with his notepad as Lazar sits next to him with a bottle of vodka "A plan?" Alex smiles "More of a what we need, I wouldn't mind having some sort of weapons ready for when we go out further after hearing whatever that was outside but we'll need to make clay moulds" Lazar tilts his head slightly which reminds Alex of a cat or a dog when they find something interesting "Or wooden moulds since the melting point is slow low wood should hold it" scribbling his last entry out Alex changes clay to wood deciding it would be easier "Let's wake Nikita and Sacha so we can get some sleep we've a lot to do in the morning"

As Nikita grudgingly gets up and sits on the nearest rock, Sacha swears at Lazar and goes to join Nikita as Alex and Lazar get as comfy as they can on the cave floor and eventually fall asleep. Alex set an alarm on his watch for 8am wanting to keep some sort of normal and needing to see when sunrise is and try to work out the length of days on the planet. As Alex and Lazar sleep Nikita and Sacha start talking about who might be on the planet and more importantly what they think of Alex, Nikita is currently sitting on the fence, while Sacha despite being thankful of having freedom has a severe lack of trust when it comes to Alex, the news of others being here hasn't gone down that great with him, which considering what they left behind is understandable, the threat of being trapped by another group is terrifying to all of them. It's Alex that's having the nightmares though, nightmares about his parents, nightmares about what happened to John, nightmares about everything even Awanyu and Achak, even though none of the deaths were by his hands John Cooper, Achak and Awanyu were killed because of his actions, his screams wake himself and everyone else awake half an hour before his alarm was due to go off, sitting in a puddle of sweat, it's Lazar that goes over to see if he's OK the rest just look on, giving Alex his first view of how much they distrust him, Rada has started boiling some water for coffee, being careful not to use more than enough for a coffee each. Alex takes the time to sort himself out a little and goes to join the rest when the coffee is ready.

As they all sit around on rocks, even Pasha this time who is looking a lot better than anyone expected, as soon as everybody has their coffee Alex takes the opportunity to at least attempt to explain some of his actions "OK look I know things haven't gone smoothly and I have a lot to do with that, I realise I should have told you about the signs I'd seen marked, I was worried about how that would affect you which I realise now I shouldn't have kept it from you and moving forward I won't keep anything from you" Rada takes the chance to talk next "Who are John, Akach and Awanyu?"" Looking down into his hands "People that died because of my choices in pursuing answers about the rock that bought us here, I didn't kill them myself but it was because of me" at that point everyone puts their cups down and gives Alex a hug, for them they see it with the innocence of a child and they see how horrible it must be, to pursue something left by his parents and people dying because of it. Alex wipes away a few tears and thanks them all, once the group has settled again Alex gets up to check outside, 8.30am and the sun has risen above the trees, so far the night and day pattern seem about the same as Earth, but he'll keep a day by day record of it for now.

As he sits back down talk turns to a plan moving forward, with everyone in agreement about doing it the right way first time, instead of doing part of the job and having to do it all again later, Alex starts to explain his plan, starting with four people going in a group to find somewhere to set up base and taking something with them to mark their route so they don't get lost in the jungle and while they are gone the rest can sort through bags and divide up what they have into categories and choose one person to ration food and water and possibly vodka, Alex doesn't like the idea of a group of Russians without vodka. As they continue talking and working out who's doing what, Lazar, Alex, Rada and Lubov get ready to head out of the cave, Alex wanting to run a test quickly before they leave picks up the case and the rock and quickly zips it up shutting the rock away again, as the four of them stand side by side waiting, hoping they don't hear anything, the whole cave has gone deadly silent, quiet enough to hear a very faint fart from Nikita as she bent over to pick something up, which instantly breaks the silence into laughter. Alex happy enough with his test takes the rock out of the bag again "Keep this out of the bag while we're gone just in case" at that the four of them make their move Lubov has a bag of spray paint to mark the route, the others have food, water and some tools to act as weapons, a hammer and a some screwdrivers, although Alex doesn't think that would make much difference unless they meet Bob the builder in the jungle.

Walking out of the cave that fresh, clean air hits them all, something that none of them has experienced, no pollution, nothing, everything just feels untouched and unblemished by man and Alex's main plan is to keep it as pure as they can and not repeat the mistakes made on earth. Walking through the jungle heading in a straight line from the cave, Rada pulls out a compass to get a sense of direction "We're heading east don't forget that we might need it later" as they get to about the point Alex and Lazar did the day before Lubov notices some tracks on the ground "What do you think left these?" the others bend down as Alex places his hand down next to one of the paw prints "I don't know but it wasn't small we need to be careful" the others look, the print from claw the heel is almost the size of Alex's hand "We should stay quiet so we can hear anything around us" coming from Rada that's easy enough she barely talks, just remembers everything she sees.

Half an hour later the jungle starts to thin a little and the group can see a little further than two trees in the distance as they continue walking, it starts getting clearer and opens out into almost a meadow, at the edge of the trees separating them from a flat grassy area ahead is a small river, not too wide and the water isn't moving too fast, deciding just to cross they stop on the other side, miles of flat grassy land and fresh running water. As the four stand looking they can see a few animals, nothing that looks too dangerous but who knows, set out here on an alien world anything could be deadly, but they all agree on planning to move here and away from the jungle as soon as possible, it's only a three hour walk and that was taking it slow so at a normal pace that would probably cut it to two hours, even carrying what they have, the only problem would be getting set up before nightfall, but at least there's a place for them and no signs of any other intelligent life, well unless they live underground that is, but that is doubtful, but it's a big world and all the group can hope for at the moment is they are far enough away to be left alone.

CHAPTER 23

Back in Siberia the Russians are just starting to learn that there are major problems with the plant, the small team that was sent on the underground train, have reported back intense heat and radiation sickness and have been ordered not to return and push on, keeping constant radio contact they make slow progress trying to clear a path through the rubble, one man has collapsed against the wall, coughing up blood. The others keep trying to get through. After what seems like a lifetime one of them moves a chunk of concrete and finally see's through to the station. Carefully climbing through 3 of them stand on the platform looking for the 4th man, after a few minutes they head to the lift, resigning themselves to the realisation that he has collapsed. As they approach the lift, they realise that it has been sabotaged as well, radioing Petrov and explaining about the lift and the other two men, Petrov screams down the radio "I don't care climb up and don't radio me until you're in the bunker". The remaining men look at each other and the twisted metal cage that was a lift, the first man makes his way carefully into the lift shaft and starts the climb up, staring up the lift shaft they all start to wonder if they can even make the climb all the way up, just as the last man starts the climb, he coughs spraying droplets of blood over the ladder and wall and a couple of rungs higher he loses his grip and falls back down, the last two carry on the climb. About halfway up the man in front stops hanging his arms over the rung of the ladder, looking like he's having a rest, until his arms slide free and he plummets down the lift shaft barely missing the last man, who can only watch as he lands on a broken piece of metal that punched through his back and out of his chest, the only remaining man starts the climb again desperate not to meet the same fate. Reaching the bunker itself one man out of the five has made it. Making his way across the warehouse area, looking over toward the reactor entrance, no doors and bits of concrete sprayed across the floor and a billowing fire inside the room, then looking over to the corner Petrov wants him to investigate all he sees is an arm, laying on the floor. Radioing Petrov to inform him, Petrov hurls his radio at the wall of his and collapses back in his chair. Knowing he won't leave his tomb, he walks toward the dining room, spitting blood out on the way, as he enters the dining room he sees half a bottle of vodka on the table and sits drinking from the bottle, waiting for his death, after a few more minutes he collapses falling off the chair and taking his last breath laying on the cold concrete floor.

Petrov, sitting back in his chair, head in his hands, knowing that no matter what, when it comes out he gave anyone from Britain access to a secret bunker, he's a dead man, he will as the Russians say, disappear. All he can hope for now is that he can find out where they went and how. In the meantime, the bunker will be hit by an American nuclear warhead from just outside Crimea blaming the Ukraine for the strike, either way the war will escalate and it's all on Petrov's head, all because he stupid enough to allow Alex access the bunker, now all he can do is try to make sure Alex pays the price. After contacting the president and making his thoughts clear about how to slow the west down, the president makes the only play he can think of and orders Petrov's nuclear strike and orders Petrov to kill Alex Mackintosh and then put the gun in his mouth and pull the trigger.

As the nuke hits the Russians have already started the propaganda reports that something was fired from a Ukrainian base outside of Crimea, possibly nuclear but as yet unknown, the ball is rolling and nothing can stop it. As the reports start to hit the UK and USA of a possible nuclear attack, the Ukrainian president is already sending out reports that no missiles of any sort have been fired into Russian territory, the one thing the Russians have is that the confusion will buy them time. For now, there is a team of three Russians, two males and a female making their way to London, first stop Alex's parents' apartment to find out what he was doing and decide on their next move, no one has time to waste, it won't take long for the world to find out the Russians fired a nuke to cover something bigger up.

CHAPTER 24

In the cave things are moving along at a steady pace, tools and anything useful for building in one space, food and drink in another and a decision that until they can work out how to make clothes, all clothes should be shared by the group. Zeno a short, bald, 36-year-old man is sitting on a rock in front of all the food and drink writing down everything they have, which he's starting to realise really isn't much so they will need to hunt sooner than he'd hoped. Galina has taken the initiative and found some reasonable size bits of wood laying about just outside the cave and has started trying to make a mould for a blade of some sort, it would seem that out of the group she's very good at working with her hands, being one of the younger of the group at 32 and standing at what must be just over 6 foot, she makes a lot of the others look like one of the umper lumpers from Charlie and chocolate factory, as she finishes the mould, a short blade with an obvious handle, she stands and takes one the hammers and something to act as a chisel and starts trying to collect some of the blue metal from the cave walls, which is surprisingly easy, the rock around it is quite brittle making it easy. The others are busy doing their own things, only Nikita is paying attention to what Galina is doing and as she approaches the fire with a metal bucket full of stones containing the metal, Nikita comes over to join her "What are you making?" Galina passes the wooden mould over "I'm seeing if I can make some small blades for us it might take me a while" a smile from Nikita as she passes the mould back "Take your time we'll need them" Galina looks over the top of the bucket to see liquid metal has separated from the stone, now all she needs to do is avoid getting stone in the mould, looking around she finds a cover for one of the ventilators at the bunker, which should be fine for the purpose, taking a second bucket she places the mesh cover on top and empties the contents of the bucket from the fire over it, breathing a sigh of relief as her plan works,, now she has a bucket with just metal in which is starting to go solid again so she places if on fire again. A few minutes later and she has a bucket of liquid metal again and carefully fills the mould and sets the bucket down on the floor, sitting on her rock almost in a trance as she looks down at the mould with the metal slowly going solid, a mesmerising almost pearlescent blue, with swirls down the blade edge.

As soon as the metal has cooled enough,

she carefully removes it from the wood and holds it by the handle, it's nice and light but will need sharpening but it's a start. In the back of the cave by the fire Sacha is checking on Pasha, as he removes the dressing his smile fades, trying avoid Pasha seeing any concern on his face he turns and waves for Nikita to come over. As soon as she looks all the colour in her face drains away, the wound is infected and the skin around the area his arm was severed looks like its necrotic, if they don't do something soon they might not have time to stop it, but they have limited first aid and by the looks of it limited time. Nikita starts redressing his arm not letting on how bad it is and takes Sacha to one side. Sacha a 31-year-old, who has always had an interest in medicine "We need to do something quick or he'll go downhill before we have chance, have you any ideas?" Sacha looks down and shuffles his feet, to most people it would look like a man who's feeling uncomfortable but after 5 years stuck in a bunker with him Nikita knows this is Sacha thinking, just as Nikita starts to get annoyed waiting Sacha snaps out of his trance and grabs an empty bag "I'll be back soon I need to go and see what's out there, see if there's anything we could use" Nikita warns him to be careful and stay close to the cave which Sacha just waves off and walks out of the door into the jungle.

    Standing looking all around, he's never seen

anything like it, from what he can remember of the small town outside Moscow that once was home, if you can call the streets a home, concrete buildings all very Soviet Union looking industrial buildings and then Moscow and the academy. The academy had trees and green spaces, but he's never seen so much life, the shades of the leaves on the trees are a mix of purple, some lighter some darker, reds and greens, the plants by his feet are like nothing he's ever seen either in a book or with his own eyes. For once he gets to see what life really looks like. Just as he bends down to inspect one of the plants he hears a low growl from behind the trees, whatever it is doesn't sound big but it's hard to judge when he can't see it, deciding it would probably be wiser to pick what he can for now and get back inside the cave, quickly looking at the plants he takes a few that almost look like a balloon on a stick, no leaves on the stalks and globe like flowers on top, as he touches the stalk ready to pick one, the globe like flower suddenly opens releasing a powdery substance in the air. As he moves back away from the plant, worried in case it's poisonous , he sees the animal that was making the noise, a strange looking thing about the height of a labrador puppy, black fur, on its neck at the base of its skull a white thrill that looks like bone, maybe some sort of defence to protect its neck from attack, as it looks up and sniffs the air all Sacha can see is almost a racoon looking face, black rings circling it's eyes and inquisitive eyes. As the pair sit looking at each other for a couple of minutes, it starts moving closer, Sacha stays still as he is until its right in front of him, slowly reaching forward with an open hand expecting it to run or bite him, it just sits down in front of him and lets him pet him. With Sacha realising he's safe and doesn't need to worry about it, he plucks a couple of the balloon like flowers and a few others that are around and turns to walk back to the cave, once he gets to the wooden door, he spots the animal right behind him, seemingly content just to follow Sacha, trying to shoo the animal off doesn't work and it follows him in, a couple of small shrieks from the women as they see it, but everyone relaxes a little when it just goes to the back of the cave and lays down by the fire.

Sacha heads back to Nikita who has redressed Pasha's arm now and shows her what he's got "It isn't much to work with and we really only have one way to test any of it" Nikita turns around looking worried "What do you mean? Trial and error on a human?" nodding Sacha explains the problem, he has no equipment or anything to test it with, so all he can do is try to make something and hope it works, Nikita drops her voice almost to a whisper trying to avoid Pasha hearing "If that's what you need to do, you need to try it, we can't risk anymore of us getting ill and if it doesn't work or we don't try he's probably going to be dead anyway" Sacha sits with a bowl and the plants he gathered , picking up a small rock to use as a mortar and pestle, as he starts crushing flowers adding a little water to make it like a paste that he can put on pasha's, he hears a noise behind him, turning round he looks over to Nikita who is trying to lay Pasha down, he's having a seizure of some sort and a violent one at that. If they're not careful they lose him right now. All Sacha can do is hope this paste works and runs over with the bowl in his hands, scooping a hand full of it as Nikita lays Pasha on his side to avoid him choking on his own vomit Sacha carefully removes the bandage only to see that the black necrotic looking area has spread and is almost up to his neck, the veins on his neck are turning black which can only mean it's in the bloodstream, not wasting any more time Sacha coats the stump where his arm was once attached in the paste, now all they can do is wait and hope. None of them are particularly religious but now might be a good time to pray. Pasha has stopped having seizures at least for now and seems to be asleep, with no idea how long any healing will take if it heals with the paste at all, it was basically a lucky dip grab some plants make a paste and pray for a miracle, Sacha wouldn't give it a million to one shot of this working.

Alex and his small group have started the walk back, knowing which way they got there by the markings on the trees the walk back shouldn't take as long to get back to the cave, 2 and a half hours there so hopefully about 2 hours to get back, the animals have been fairly quiet and kept away for now, not really a surprise with a group of 4 beings they have probably never seen the likes of or at maybe never, as they walk through they start losing the markings on the trees and stop dead needing to find the markings again, as they look around Rada grabs Alex's arm and points to a tree off to the side, walking closer Alex see's what she was pointing at another marking on a tree, A triangle with a circle in the middle again standing on the spot and looking around for anymore markings on trees, Alex wonders if they could be marking a path to somewhere or something, seeing nothing from where he's standing he walks 10 steps forward and then back to where he was and repeats another three times. It's the fourth time that he finds another heading north. Walking a little further he sees another, almost in a straight line from the first two, turning around and almost jumping in the air not realising Rada was right behind him looking worried "It's OK Rada we know what direction they seem to be so for now we'll avoid that way, let's get back and find our markings" just as they get back to the other two who have found the markings they start the rest of the walk back as Alex explains about the other markings, as he starts telling them he realises the markings were only on one side of the tree so they must be in the north, so that way is a no go area for now, hopefully whoever or whatever it is won't see their markings.

As the group finally start following their own markings and start moving again, there's a sudden noise to one side of them, something not all that different to a hedgehog only bigger probably the size of a small dog, thankfully it keeps walking, Alex isn't wanting to see what the spines are or whether there poisonous. The team speed up easily finding the markings and not seeing much of anything else, it doesn't take them long to get back to the cave and back to safety. As the group sit down, Alex stays standing "We need a plan, we can't stay here much longer, we've seen trees with markings on and from what I can work out it seems to be marking a path between us and a meadow area that we have found, I think we should have a group head for the meadow with tools to start making a shelter, it'll have to be done during daylight hours I don't want anyone out at night yet, maybe 6 people to build a shelter secure enough and big enough for us all to be able to sleep in while we start plans for a permanent settlement, the clearing has running water and animals around to hunt" Zeno raises his hand, not much different from a child needing to use the toilet "For fuck sake Zeno put your damn hand down" a laugh from the rest as Zeno playfully punches Nikita on the arm "We have good rations for about a week or not so good rations for 2 weeks so I'd suggest getting started as soon as we can, but we do have vodka for about 3 weeks" Nikita laughs "Well we could ration for 2 weeks and stay drunk, we won't notice it as much" at that a bottle of vodka appears like magic courtesy of Lazar.

As the group sit and have a drink, no one really caring what time it is anymore, it's not like they have a reactor to run anymore. As they sit Lazar starts splitting people into groups which Alex is happy to leave him to do, he has no idea of anyone's skill sets, it's not long before they have a group of builders, a couple of cooks and medics on hand if anyone gets crushed cutting trees down drunk. As the sun starts to get low and everyone winds down for the night, with some sort of plan for the coming days, Alex pulls out his notepad to jot down sunset, looking at the page of his notepad with a look of confusion, Nikita leans over his shoulder "The days are getting shorter?" Alex nods glumly "Half an hour shorter than yesterday, we need to be careful" Nikita puts a gentle hand on his shoulder "I saw a set of radios over there we could check the range tomorrow that way we can at least call them back from the campsite if we need to, since we won't be able to follow times if the sunset keeps shifting" Alex nods and puts a hand on Nikitas, then quickly pulls it away, he's always been a little awkward around women, well awkward would be an understatement he hasn't been with anyone for years. Nikita stands up pulling him up and leading him to the cave entrance, standing at the open door they both stand and watch the sunset through a small clearing in the tree canopy, watching quietly it's Nikita that spots it "Is that another planet?" Watching Alex trying to see where she's looking she points "Just to the left side of the sun, it doesn't look like a moon" Finally seeing it, he stands staring almost unable to take his eyes away until they start hearing noises, a low guttural howl comes from the left of them, followed by more, from almost every direction, they take the hint and go back into the cave closing the door and locking it with a crow bar.

Heading back to the group who are now whispering between themselves and pointing at Nikita and Alex, Nikita throws piece of food at Lazar "hui" Lazar laughs "Why do you always blame me woman", "Because it's always you" sitting with the group having a drink, Alex looks around at a group of smiling Russians, chatting, joking and drinking, acting like they haven't got a care in the world, free for the first time. Alex on the other hand is putting on a good show, but he's not as happy as the rest, coming here came at a price, 3 people died for him to get here, the reactor will be in full meltdown and probably cost even more life and depending on how the Russian's deal with it, the cost of life could be high. He hasn't been sleeping well and has tried to make sure he's not close to anyone in an attempt to avoid his nightmares being noticed, the group know already that people died and are happy to blame the Kremlin for that. Then of course there's the classified information he gave to Petrov Nikitin to gain access to the reactor, information that could easily start a war.

CHAPTER 25

Back in Siberia things are going from bad to worse, the nuclear strike hit the bunker, which not only added to the amount of radiation, but was also picked up straight away by satellites, the main blast door to the bunker has also been compromised, allowing a flow of radiation to escape the bunker. Petrov has sent all the information Alex handed over to the Kremlin, maybe in some vain hope to save his own life. The information about the NASA plan to put the ISS out of operation and not tell Russia to get there men out has not gone down well and a plan to sabotage the space station is in the process of being finalised, they intend to do it by way of bringing their cosmonauts home following a death of a family member and on the way out they will sabotage the station. It becomes evident that war is inevitable.

Petrov's attempts at finding Alex and everyone else that were at the bunker have come up with nothing, well apart from a severed arm, no sign of anyone in the bunker and now he can't find anything else out the men that had been sent have all died and the train is just as dead, the only way in is either clear a path and walk from the tunnel collapse, assuming they can even run a second train down the tunnel, the only other way is a helicopter to the bunker blast door, but with the radiation levels so high, not even the protective gear available would be enough. This leaves Petrov with one last solution, send another missile in some hope of collapsing the mountain and sealing off the bunker, unless his scientists can come up with something,

America have started getting reports of increasing radiation levels in Alaska and Canada, with governments issuing warnings to civilians to stay at hope and lock all doors and windows, which has started a mass panic causing shops to be emptied of food and anything else people think they'll need, the full news of what is happening hasn't been released to the public yet but it won't take long. As the shops run empty the looting has begun, even in the most respectful towns the locals have been stealing anything they can. Meanwhile the Whitehouse is desperately trying to work out exactly what it is happening with reports coming out of Russia claiming the nuke was American, a story that the Whitehouse is denying, I mean why wouldn't they, at the time of the blast they didn't know anything about Alex

Mackintosh, John Cooper, two native Americans or even evidence of a secret nuclear reactor in Siberia, although there had been stories for years, Siberia is huge so tracking down one bunker in the side of a mountain was near on impossible.

America has been desperately trying to have open communications with the Kremlin with no luck at all and panic has started to set in, this has the prospect of being an even bigger risk than the cold war and anything either side does has to be done carefully. Satellite images and thermal imaging images are showing a huge zone in Siberia tracking toward Alaska and Canada and scientists are predicting that eventually the cloud of radiation will reach Vancouver in the next 36 hours and Los Angeles in the next 48 hours, the biggest problem is how do they evacuate massive areas of America, with all models showing that the radiation will continue spewing out of the bunker for years if not sealed in some way and that the cloud of radiation depending on weather patterns has the prospect to affect the planet not just Canada and America.

With every world government except Russia in communication and trying to reach an agreement on what could be done, if anything can be done. For Russia they are on the ball, it's obvious that Russia can do nothing, they are not going to tell their people that Russia will be blanketed by radiation within hours, barely anyone knows, the president, Petrov Nikitin and hand full on military personal. There is no time to get anyone home from the ISS and no way of evacuating Siberia and Russia and nothing they can do to save anyone, so orders have been sent to the two Russian cosmonauts on the ISS to trigger an explosion aboard the space station, something big enough to scatter debris in some hope of taking out as many satellites as possible.

No one is even paying attention to the ISS and with everything else happening around the world no one's even talking to them at the time that three separates explosions rip apart the space station, sending everyone on board into space, there isn't even time to talk to NASA, one explosion in the US Lab in the centre of the space station tearing the station in two, another in node 2 that connects the Japanese module and another in node 1 that connects the station to the joint airlock, with a massive amount of damage causing debris to spew out everywhere, on board no one stood a chance, the cloud of debris will hit almost every satellite in orbit, causing a massive chain reaction, one satellite breaks into a million pieces taking out several other ones and the chain reaction grows and grows. Just as the first explosion was detonated, an ex-KGB agent is sat in his office with a pistol in one hand and a bottle of vodka in the other, taking a mouth full of vodka Petrov Nikitin puts the gun to his temple, swallows his vodka and pulls the trigger, sending a spray of blood and brain across the room, decorating the wall like a Jackson Pollock painting. He knew when this went wrong that he was dead this way he did it on his own terms, there's so much panic around the Kremlin that no one even heard the gun shot.

As news filters through to the Whitehouse about the ISS a joint call is made with all NATO countries requesting a joint decision on firing nuclear weapons at Russia. Not one country votes no, a unilateral vote on the use of nuclear warheads against Russia, America is first to press that big red button, the big red button that has been at every past presidents use since Oppenheimer's work, but hasn't been pressed since Hiroshima, has now been pressed with Americas warhead targeting Moscow, what was it Oppenheimer said? "Now I have become death, the Destroyer of worlds" as the button was pressed, the president of the great United States of America is seen sitting behind his desk in the White House with tears streaming down his face, he is and always will be the last American President.

As the Kremlin hear about the nuclear warhead heading straight to them the obvious move is made, it's always sounded like a stereotype but an accurate one, the Kremlin press their red button and if the end hadn't already begun, it has now.

CHAPTER 26

Back in their cave everyone is oblivious to anything that is happening back home, they don't even realise that are truly safe, no one can follow, not anymore but then again, they don't care anymore, any thoughts of anyone coming after them have been forgotten. Sitting around the small fire in the cave drinking coffee out of empty cans, divided in to their groups ready for the first day's proper work, Nikita goes to check on Pasha and change his dressings, now that he's talking again and feeling better, she's relaxed a little and Rada has taken over looking after him, they always had a connection, but now they are away from all the rules and no longer isolated in a bunker they can be themselves. Alex is testing the radios and making sure there is spare batteries, passing one to Lazar to take to the meadow clearing and Alex will hold on to the other one, ready to radio them when they need to come back, sunrise was at the same difference in time half an hour early, which to Alex and Nikita makes little sense at the moment.

As the teams start to separate into groups

and the builders have gone to start on the first shelter in the more permanent base, Rada and Pasha have made a sort of table and chairs from rocks to start putting together a plan for the settlement, Sacha is going through first aid equipment and Nikita and Alex are talking, out of the way of everyone else "I think we should go and find the markings on the trees and follow them for a bit, try and find out who is here and where they are, but we'll need to be careful" Nikita ponders Alex's suggestion for a minute "OK but first sign of people we head back?" Alex nods and goes to tell the others, a few mumbles of disagreement but they accept the plan anyway.

As they leave the cave, Alex leads the way back to where he saw the markings, finding the first tree he saw they lead in one direction, so that's the direction they walk slowly making their way through the trees, staying as quiet as possible, listening for anything that makes a noise, it wouldn't surprise them if the trees started making noise as well, every other step and they hear some sort of animal, but they haven't seen anything. As they walk through a little further the trees seem to shrink away, getting thinner and shorter. It doesn't take long before they start seeing faint signs of life, as they reach the point where the trees are more separated and the view forward becomes clearer, they can see another cave off to the right and further ahead what looks like a settlement, but not little log cabins or anything something much bigger, but with how clear the view and the fact that they are looking down a slight incline it must be at least 50 miles away minimum, Nikita grabs Alex's arm "We can't go down there" Alex shakes his head "No not yet but at least we know their far enough away from us to be safe, hopefully" Alex points to the cave and the pair start the walk toward it, as they approach the cave, they start to realise how much it looks like their own cave but this one has a marking just at the cave entrance, the same marking Alex saw the first time he saw through the portal "This is the first cave I saw theone I had the photo of" walking inside Nikita grabs Alex's hand out of impulse but it's Alex that gently slides his fingers through her's and gives it a gentle squeeze.

As they approach the halfway point of the cave Alex kicks something, looking down he sees a spear laying on the floor, an odd design, long wooden shaft tipped with a point that is made from one piece of metal but has several points off to the sides, this spear is made to inflict maximum damage, picking up the spear and walking further through they reach the back of the cave and Alex drops to his knees. Nikita looks at the back wall to see a skeleton pinned to the cave wall with another spear, the blades on the spear so sharp they cut several bones clean, looking closer at the skeleton she sees a medallion hanging round it's neck or what would have been a neck, gently removing it from the skeletons neck she holds it to Alex's face "You recognise this don't you?" Alex nods glumly in the dimly lit cave "It was my dad's" looking around a little more he spots broken seats from a plane and scraps of metal "This doesn't make sense, part of the plane must be here that's why they couldn't find bodies, some of it ended up here, my parents must have had another way here, maybe something they found in Peru, maybe something they went looking for in Peru, I need to have a look around the cave before we leave" Nikita heads for the corner of the cave "There's nothing here Alex just bits of cloth from plane seats and some chunks of metal from the plane" Alex calls her over "I don't think it's here if it was another rock whoever killed him probably has it and my guess would be the settlement down the hill, that can wait for now we can't risk being noticed let's take the spears and head back" Nikita steps up to Alex "Do you need a minute before we leave?" Alex shakes his head and starts walking with Nikita following behind.

Back in the cave everyone is gathered toward the back of the cave all looking down at the ground, as Alex and Nikita arrive back and walk toward them, they all part so that Alex and Nikita can see Pasha, having a seizure and sweating profusely "What happened?" the first and most obvious question came from Alex as Nikita kneels down and places the back of her hand on Pasha's forehead "He's burning up" Sacha kneels at the side of Nikita "His temperature is up at 43 he won't survive long like this and nothing we have is bringing it down, he's been having seizures for about half an hour on and off, it must be sepsis can we talk in private?" Nikita, Alex, and Sacha walk toward the cave entrance looking out of the open door "Wait it's getting dark let me radio the group in the clearing first" it takes less than a minute for Alex to radio and get the team heading back, Sacha is looking white as a sheet "There's nothing we can do for him" Nikita slumps down against the wall "What do we do? I don't want everyone to have see him go like this" the three of them sit, barely making a sound, it's Sacha who vocalises what the other two are thinking "The only thing I can think is we take him outside but the group will have to be told what we're doing" Just at that point they hear the others coming "Let's wait with Pasha and everyone can say their goodbyes I guess"

As they walk back and join the rest, Pasha's seizures have stopped but he's not waking up, Nikita checks his pulse and shakes he her head looking at Alex "His pulse is weak he hasn't got long and I don't think it's good for us to have to watch him go like this, we should put his body outside the cave tonight and if he's still there in the morning we will make sure he is buried I'm sorry but we see no other choice" the group silently agree, the team from the clearing were just in time to hear everything" as everyone says their goodbyes Alex and Sacha get ready to move him, as people move away they lift Pasha and carefully carry him out of the cave, leaning him against a tree a little distance away, and make their way back. As soon as they get in the cave Sacha grabs some vodka and Alex starts playing music on what little battery his phone has left, in some attempt to mask the inevitable noise from outside when whatever is out there finds Pasha.

As night falls and Alex jots the time down in his notepad, the same again 30 minutes earlier than the day before, by his working they have about a week before morning and night meet, which isn't exactly filling Alex with optimism, sitting with music playing and vodka being passed around he jots a note with his theory and passes it to Nikita "Sunrise and sunset are changing, it's 30 minutes earlier getting darker and 30 minutes later getting light, if I'm right in about a week it will just be night and then work the other way round so night and day will switch, so every 24 days night and day will switch" Nikita sits looking at the note, confused and worried and scribbles one word "Fuck". Alex sits trying to work out how many days they have before darkness stops them doing anything, the music is loud which is good because Alex has already started to hear noise outside the cave thankfully the music is masking it from the others, who at the moment at least half of them are a little tipsy, a sight Alex would have liked to avoided normally but taking into consideration what has happened, he'd rather see them drunk for one night. Finally finishing working out how much time they have which is looking like 5 days, 5 days to get a shelter built, he doesn't want to be trapped in this cave when it hits.

Just as he gets up to walk back to the group, he hears some louder noises outside, turning and looking at the group no one has noticed anything, as he moves closer to wall blocking the cave entrance off, he hears what sounds like Pasha's body being dragged away, which although he would have preferred to give him a burial, this makes things easier, not only time wise, but less trauma for the group, who so far seem to be dealing with it a lot better than he expected, they've been drinking and sharing stories, an activity that Alex doesn't really feel he fits into. Heading back to the group with some sort of plan, Alex grabs the vodka and addresses the group "We have 5 days to get a shelter built, day and night will switch and we will have at least one day of total darkness and I'd rather be out of here by then so in the morning we all go to the clearing, we'll take as much as we can carry, the days are short now so we need to work fast, essentials first the rest we can come back to, but I'd rather not stay another night in this cave" everyone agrees with the customary banging of drink containers although it's a little dull not having a table to bang them on or glasses to drink from, but Alex got the message.

Thoughts of his father's skeleton and the spears they bought back have been all but forgotten in all the chaos of what happened with Pasha, until Alex turns to look around the cave and sees the two spears leaning against the cave wall. Carefully not wanting to upset the group anymore and with the help of Nikita they tell the group about their morbid discovery, as the questions begin with people being more intrigued than upset, but they didn't know his father and as the conversation goes on Alex realises just how little he knew about his father, a name and some postcards and letters, William Mackintosh sender of postcards, at least that's what would probably be put on his headstone, the questions pour out, why didn't the animals take the body? Where is his mum? Who killed him? Why did they kill him? And the biggest one who killed him? Alex tells them about the settlement they saw from the cave entrance and the agreement is 100% in favour of staying away until they are at least settled and more prepared.

As the night goes on and people start to get tired they all start finding spaces to sleep and settling down, Alex can only assume that Pasha's body has been taken away, one by one the group of slightly drunk Russians fall asleep, Alex on the other hand is having an unsettled night, his mind racing with questions and nightmares of what he has done and the list of deaths that he feels responsible for, John Cooper, Awanyu, Achak, Pasha, but he has blood on his hands that much he does know. As he looks around the group of sleeping Russians, he also starts to realise something else, he has given these people something they would have never had, freedom, pure and simple freedom. Whether that negates some of the guilt for the people that have died is another matter entirely.

Just as Alex starts to fall asleep, a huge bang on the wooden wall wakes everyone up, with a few squeals from the women and some of the men, they all sit in silence, waiting to see if it happens again, another huge bang on the wall, louder than before and some of the group jump into action, Alex and Nikita grabbing a spear each the others grabbing whatever they can find to defend themselves with. A third huge bang on the wall splinters on of the wooden beams, showing a small opening and a small glimpse of fur, something that looks quite big. It's Alex that takes his chance and runs straight at it with the spear, thrusting the spear forward and through the gap, it slides effortlessly into the side of the animal, as the animal bucks and runs the spear stays stuck in its side with Alex holding the other end and drags him crashing into the wall headfirst.

Nikita runs straight to Alex who is lying flat on his back with his hands holding his head, blood coming from a cut on his forehead and more than a little dazed, Sacha comes over carrying a first aid kit and starts cleaning up and patching Alex's forehead. Sitting against the wooden wall Alex starts laughing "Well the spears are good need to make me some more of those and a helmet, but I'm not spending another night here whatever that is knows we're here now and isn't afraid of the rock, the suns starting to come up let's get our stuff together"

CHAPTER 27

With the team loaded with bags, having managed to get everything in one go, the trip might be slow but they won't have to come back, at least that's one thing but by Alex's working out they have about 4 days to get the shelter built and some defences, but he has a plan for that. Leaving the confines of the cave, hopefully for the last time with Alex carrying his weight in supplies and the rock in its lead lined coffin, where he plans to leave it, they walk straight for the clearing following the trees marked out to show the way, two hours later they start to see the trees thinning and hearing running water from the river separating them from the meadow, to Alex's relief the group of builders have made a kind of bridge to save going through the water. As soon as he can see the place they've been building, his face changes from tired and plain, to amazed and excited, they have already built the majority of a shelter large enough to offer a safe place to sleep, all that's missing is the roof and some defences.

Nikita takes the bags from Alex and drops

them on the floor "Look at me and follow my finger", as Nikita checks him over and realises, he has concussion from hitting his head so hard "You need to rest you have concussion" with his head pounding he doesn't have the energy or will to fight her. Sitting down on a rock as the rest of the team get to building, he starts to think about defences and that blue metal, they could use it to make spears and dig them in at angle around the shelter, a little like roman defences. Alex calls a few of them over, Sacha, Rada and Oksana and explains his idea, the only change so far will be that they'll make wooden spears for now until they have time to mine some of the metal. Alex supports the decision because there isn't really another way but it leaves him nervous, whatever was trying to get through the wall at the cave was big and having a full day in darkness there's likely to be more than just one.

Just as it starts getting a little darker a group of sweaty tired builders walk over to Alex "We're done let's all get inside, how's your head?" slowly getting up still feeling a little light headed Alex smiles "It's still here I think" as they walk over and step inside the shelter, Alex notices the wooden spears all dug into the ground at angles pointing up, looking at them it might be enough for now, but Alex would be happier with a second row, just for safety but they can work on the that in the morning, well afternoon now since it's darker for longer. Walking into the shelter Alex and Nikita are amazed at how well it's been built and secured, even the beast from the cave would have trouble breaking in, Alex walks to the back and finds a place to lie down "I'm just going to try and get some rest my heads throbbing" at that Nikita gives him a small peck on the cheek and turns away blushing.

The rest of the group quietly discuss plans, trying to keep the noise down for Alex, all feeling lucky its only concussion and nothing more serious, they've already planned the next two or three days and then they will be hunkering down and although none of them are religious, they'll probably spend a lot of that time praying. They have a hunting group to get some fresh meat, people to collect and boil water for drinking, a couple of people to try and make some form of furniture and a safe place to have a fire inside, that could be a challenge, but they've overcome worse obstacles. Nikita is happy that their all keeping busy, they haven't had time to think about losing Pasha and that at least means they'll stay focused on the important parts, they can all mourn later for now it's about survival.

CHAPTER 28

Back on earth as the news starts to come out that the planet is all but dead, the bunker business has really picked up and the doomsday planners feel somewhat smug now, world governments have taken it upon themselves to open military bunkers to set groups of people, coldly choosing who can live and who can die, filling the bunkers, firstly with what they believe is needed and any spare spaces being sold to the highest bidders, even at the end their still at their core are corrupt. The one thing a small minority realise is that even these doomsday bunkers that have been kitted out for everything will not be enough to sustain people for the length of time needed, some may survive but it will be a hard long winter. Preparations are already being hampered by looting, mass fires and fighting in the streets, that's just in the places where people are still alive, there have been 30 nuclear weapon launches around since this is all began and world governments seem to want to just fire everything.

The worst hit areas have all but been wiped

out and if the people didn't die straight away it won't be long before they do, Russia has been one of the hardest hit areas and America a close second, Moscow was hit first but before the nuke hit, they launched at Washington and New York, paralysing America, and forces those who could hide into hiding, there isn't expected to be many survivors from the blast and even less from the fallout. Luckily for those no longer on the planet they know none of this, especially Alex, having the worlds blood on his hands might be a little too much. Some of the world's government have survived so far and have managed to get in government-controlled bunkers, but with no communications due to the rapid fallout from the ISS exploding into a million pieces and talking out 95% of the worlds satellites, they have no way of communicating with the outside world and are now oblivious to the destruction outside. China has managed to stay out of most of it, which has been a surprise for most but their close proximity to Russia has meant that they are still doomed, there is nowhere that is safe. It's been 3 days since Alex and the others vanished and no one even knows, there is no one to miss them and no one that knows that there was a chance to escape this, but then again if it hadn't been for Alex taking his group with him in the first place this would never have happened.

In Australia news has made it through but they have more time to plan and a group of doomsday planners, one of the biggest groups in the world, had actually made a clear plan for just this eventuality. They have a fully stocked bunker, well set of bunkers, 10 in total all linked by tunnels, air filters and purifiers set up throughout, everything they need to survive for at least 20 years and they already had their list of survivors, mainly built up from people that paid into the project, but scientists, doctors anyone and everyone that could be useful and enough space and supplies for 300 people, enough to restart a population and well not to put it too bluntly a breeding program and not just for the animals. They have already worked out a sustainable system for repopulating and training up the next generation of survivors, survivors that will be born in bunkers, a little like a zoo, bred in captivity for set purposes. Now we think about it, this is going to be no better than the secret academy in Russia.

4 days into a nuclear war and the war is over, even if there are nukes still there's no one left to launch them. The Australians have sealed themselves in, China has been decimated as with most of the world now, a few bunkers spread out that could survive a few years of nuclear winter but not much more than that. In four days the

world has crumbled, thousands of years to build and evolve, undone in four days, it seems hard to believe, but true. The majority of scientists always believed that the next extinction level event would be caused by humans, so now there are two sets of survivors on two separate planets, completely oblivious to each other.

CHAPTER 29

Back at their new settlement, the days are becoming shorter making daily work harder, but they have found their own routines, first light the hunting party heads out and have managed to gather some meat, a smoker has been built in a separate room joined to the shelter to cure the meat for longevity and they enough water to last about a week, which is good considering the vodka is starting to run out, but Lazar has been busy making moonshine in the corner of the shelter and Alex has already decided he won't be the first one to try it. They have about two days where they will have any daylight, so daily tasks are being finished until the long night is over, they have a day with one hour of daylight and the next will be 30 minutes, then darkness, hopefully one day, but it's hard to know for certain, time will tell.

Alex's concussion lasted two days and while he was waiting for it to pass, he and Rada sit looking at the plans she made for the settlement with Pasha, a cabin each, the current shelter to be turned into a meeting area and social area, defences around each building and around the main camp, it will take a lot of work, but they have all the time in the world.

As the last night starts to end, they all sit outside, they've set fires burning around the camp, more to see what happens than actually believing they will help, as the light starts to fade again, they head inside and block the door shut with a thick beam and logs through small holes in the floor, wedged against the door. As they sit around there isn't much talking, just sitting listening, the previous nights since they've been at the shelter have been a lot quieter than the jungle was, the animals they have seen have been smaller and more timid and haven't been trying to rip their heads off. Things remain quiet for a little while and a few have actually managed to get to sleep.

It's Galina that hears the first noises, faint noises in the distance, as she alerts the others they sit listening and then from nowhere a huge guttural roar, nothing they've ever heard before, not here and not on earth. As the distant noises start getting closer the roar turns into several roars, as if there is about to be a battle outside, the group have all shrank into one corner of the shelter, only Alex and Nikita are still standing near the door, listening and whispering to each other trying not to worry the rest. Just as Alex is certain something is going to try to get in the shelter, they hear shouts from the direction of the other settlement and animal noises, injured animal noises. Then silence, but they're not alone.

Unsure what to do next Alex and Nikita stand by the door, the rest of them are gingerly moving out of the corner, Alex thought it was odd that they all acted like that, like children terrified by an abusive parent, then he remembered they have known nothing of the outside world, the fact they have made it this far has been a shock, it's so easily forgotten, the life they had or more to the point, the life they didn't have. As things settle outside, they hear footsteps approaching the door. Alex and Nikita stand listening, straining to hear anyone talking and then both fly backwards as someone knocks on the door. Staring at each other not sure what to do Alex steps forward "Hello?", "Could we come in as you know it's not safe out here" Alex signals to the rest to stay quiet as he and Nikita slowly move the logs and then lift the bar sealing the door. Slowly opening the door to peek outside he sees three men, native American in appearance, but not native American at the same time.

Opening the door and allowing the three men inside, Alex notices whatever it is they rode in on, something odd looking, for some reason he expected horses, but these are stocky built muscular animals, shoulder height to one of the men, but the men are also taller, are they men? The height may be the difference in gravity. As the third man steps in he blocks the door up for safety, or to make it harder for the group to leave, "We are not here to harm you, merely welcome you" Alex ushers the men to a bench that's been made "Where exactly is this?"

"That's an easy question to answer, this planet we name Xero, it was here before earth and will remain after, the first people on earth came from here, we have been known by many names but the one that has stuck with us through time is Anasazi or ancient ones, but we prefer Anasazi, we have through time tried to help mankind on earth, but that has always ended the same way, war, greed and violence. The tools we helped build are turned into weapons, having belief spread religion, which created wars of its own, so we left and came back here to our ancestral home, leaving earth to destroy itself, we will not turn you away and we will help but if there are problems from earth that you bring with you, we will have to take action"

"So we are free here?"

"Yes, on agreement that you will not try to attack us and that you pass the portal stone to us now, we can't risk you using it again"

Alex walks over and picks up the lead lined case and hands it over, only one has spoken the other two seem more like guards than dignitaries "Thank you we will make our way home" before they get to leave Alex has one question "I found my father's skeleton in a cave not far away, with one of those spears through him can you at least tell me why he was killed?"

"That was unfortunate, we tried to help him but he killed one of ours and would have killed more if we didn't do something, I am sorry it was your father"

Passing Alex a piece of paper the men leave the shelter and climb on their animals and move away, heading back toward the settlement Alex and Nikita had seen. The note itself simply read "Please accept an invite to come see our elders when you have settled and have enough daylight to make it here safely"

As Alex passes the note around to the group and they all sit talking, things have fallen silent outside as Alex passes a bottle of vodka around.

WELCOME TO PLANET XERO

Printed in Great Britain
by Amazon